BOUNCER

BAD BOYS IN BIG TROUBLE 2

FIONA ROARKE

BOUNCER
Bad Boys in Big Trouble 2

Nickel Road Publishing
ISBN: 978-1-944312-03-9

Published in the United States of America

DEDICATION

For all the folks near and far who have helped me with this book. Thank you.

DEA Agent Reece Langston has spent a year at the city's hottest club, working his way closer to the core of a money laundering operation. Women throw themselves at him all the time, but there's only one he's interested in catching. And she won't even tell him her name.

FBI Agent Jessica Hayes doesn't know much about the sexy stranger except that he's tall, dark and gorgeous. Best of all, he seems just as drawn to her as she is to him—in other words, he's the perfect man to show one kick-ass virgin what sex is all about. No names, no strings and no regrets. Their one-night stand turns into two. Then a date. Then…maybe more.

Everything is going deliciously well until Jessica's boss orders her to use her lover to further an FBI operation.

Everything is going deliciously well until Reece's handler orders him to use his lover to get closer to his target.

Is their desire enough to match the danger and deception?

Bouncer, Bad Boys in Big Trouble 2
Nothing's sexier than a good man gone bad boy.

PROLOGUE

Saturday night – Joe's Bar

"What do you mean you've never had sex before?" The utter surprise in Kelli Baker's tone was second only to the volume at which she shouted the inflammatory information.

Jessica Hayes sent her soon-to-be-*ex*-best friend a horrified look. Speechless, she promptly lowered her head in abject shame, afraid to look around and see who might have heard the notification to the world of her virginal status. The trendy upscale bar they were in was quiet enough that voices could definitely carry well outside of their private two person circle.

Knowing Kelli as she did and that her friend would continue chattering until stopped, Jessica regrouped quickly and snapped, "Could you say that a little louder? I don't think the single desperate men of Outer Mongolia heard you."

Kelli glanced over one shoulder quickly and promptly touched Jessica's hand in apology. "Well, I'm sorry, but I mean, damn, girlfriend! When you said you *really* needed to get laid I didn't realize we were talking

1

about the premier event. I almost brought a guy with me tonight, but he had to work. So how did you make it to your advanced age without bumping uglies with a guy?"

"Four older brothers and a small Midwestern town." Jessica took a sip of her club soda with lime and the memories of her high school years invaded her thoughts.

The high school boys of Cornelia, Missouri were all cowards. No guy would ever ask her out for fear of retribution. Her shortest brother was six foot two, damn it. A mother bear seemed neglectful in comparison to her brothers and the way they protected her from the advances of any male in a three county radius, a skill they learned well from their father.

Even now she couldn't visit home without all the eligible bachelors between the ages of eighteen and eighty cowering away from her in fear.

"You don't say. Sounds like the title of a bad TV movie of the week."

"Yeah, that's my love life—a bad TV movie of the week broadcast on cable at two in the morning. It isn't as if I haven't tried, you know. I got close a couple of times, but in retrospect I was far too picky."

"Define close," Kelli said, twirling her drink straw around the ice in the bottom of her nearly empty glass.

"My second year of college."

"Do tell."

"He was a sports media major. Deep voice. Sexy deep-blue eyes. He stared at me in the cafeteria for a month before finally asking me out."

"So why didn't you do him?"

"I tried. We went to a pledge week frat party at his fraternity house, where he managed to get rip-roaring drunk in record time. He led me, staggering all the way, to his room. We had to kick out another couple and he cleared most of the coats off the bed before feeling me

2

up a couple times and then ejaculating on the sleeve of one unlucky guest's Burberry jacket."

"Eew. That's just nasty."

"Oh, I'm so sorry to offend your delicate sensibilities. It was a frat party. Everyone knows you take your chances if you leave coats and stuff laying around in any of the bedrooms. That was karma, pure and simple."

"So you didn't even get anything out of the near exchange of bodily fluids?"

"Not really. I got up and left, but quite a few people saw me leave his bedroom. Frat Boy apparently thought he did the deed, so he washed his hands of me directly afterwards and considered the conquest done. On Monday he started staring at a freshman with big boobs and ignored me completely. I was so embarrassed. It took me a year and a half to get up enough nerve to try again."

Kelli shook her head. "He's the one who should have been embarrassed. I wish I'd been around back then to get you back up on the horse." She took a long sip, finished her drink and gestured at the busy bartender to prepare another. "As a matter of fact, if you'd mentioned I was dealing with virgin territory tonight, I would have selected a different place. Hell, I would have hand-picked someone special to take care of you."

The thought of Kelli explaining to *someone special* how her friend needed to be de-virginized made Jessica wish she'd ordered tequila tonight instead of club soda to numb the humiliation.

"Great. Or I could just schedule an appointment with my gynecologist and have it done surgically. Maybe she could light a candle for atmosphere."

"No way. Don't do that. What about all those hunky guys with guns where you work? Surely there are possibilities there, right?"

"No. I never want to date anyone from law enforcement, and especially not anyone I work with."

"Why not?"

"Too weird to have slept with someone and then work with them, knowing what they look like naked. Besides, what if it didn't work out? Too much drama. So no, law enforcement guys are not an option. Move on."

"Fine. Then leave it to me. I'll pick someone nice, someone you won't ever see again, and most especially a guy who knows what he's doing without any guilt-filled strings attached."

"So a total stranger you know firsthand is sexually amazing? That man surely doesn't exist or you'd already have him chained to your bed. I don't need you to find anyone for me. I especially don't want someone you've been with."

"Are you sure? I know a guy or two who would volunteer in an emergency." Kelli smiled. "This seems like an emergency to me."

"Well, it's not. And really? Men you've used up and thrown away? No, thank you very much."

"It's not like that. The men I have in mind didn't work for me in other ways. Or I didn't work for them, but we remained friends. It can be done."

"So you say. Still, I'm not looking for a friend of yours to deflower me."

"I would have volunteered," said a sleazy voice from over Jessica's shoulder. A voice that sent a shard of panic to her heart. A voice she recognized from work.

Damn it all to hell.

Jessica swiveled on her bar stool, coming face-to-face Agent Neil Wiley, resident dick and infamous idiotic office lothario. After keeping a low profile these past several months since moving here from her Midwestern hometown after FBI training, Neil—also known as the bastard of the second floor—had just learned her deepest secret.

Jessica tried not to gnash her teeth in frustration. Given Neil's proclivity to gossip, she knew by Monday morning the entire FBI building would be apprised of her limited sexual expertise. Or worse, he'd hound her about it privately until she shot out his kneecaps in annoyance. Then again, the paperwork involved in firing her service weapon might just be worth it in this case.

She shouldn't care about Neil, but it was hard enough to make friends, especially male friends, in a new city without having a cloud of virginity smack dab over her head.

"As a matter of fact, I'll volunteer right now. Want to go to your place or mine so I can pop your cherry, Agent Hayes?" he asked and bit into a green olive from his martini.

CHAPTER 1

Well after midnight on a lonely street

Reece Langston fell in love with her delicious heart-shaped ass first, because that was the first part he saw. The goddess was bent over rummaging around the open trunk of her car, which sported a flat tire, muttering curses as clanking ensued.

"...stupid frickin'...ah ha! There you are!"

When she straightened and emerged clutching a tire iron in one fisted hand, he got his first look at the angelic face that went with that lovely derriere. She simply took his breath away. She was a blonde. He loved blondes. Her hair fell to her shoulders in waves. She was tall, but not overly so. She had long shapely legs attached to that gorgeous butt, and he easily pictured them wrapped around his naked, sweaty waist as he thrust endlessly... *Calm down*, he told himself.

A ferocious urge stirred in his loins, the likes of which made him look down at his own crotch in wonder. He waited, almost expecting to see his cock burst through the zipper of his jeans to take a closer look at the delectable instigator of the rampant excitement pervading the space below his belt.

It had been so long.

Reece glanced back up in time to see her squat beside the rear passenger-side tire, thrusting her ass out in his direction again. The slacks she wore hugged her lower half nicely. He had to close his eyes because the visual overwhelmed him, and wondered how best to convince the angel before him they were destined to be together.

Tonight. Now. Was her back seat big enough for the both of them?

Another glance at his mystery future lover as she applied the tire iron to the unseen jack under her car made him smile. He thought of an opening line to break the ice.

"You're doing it wrong," he told her in an overloud tone. She startled, almost lost her balance, and shot him an evil glare over one slim shoulder. He cursed his long deprived reptilian libido, realizing it was foolish to sneak up on a woman fixing a flat tire at night on a deserted street. He was lucky she hadn't just shot him through the heart, or worse, whipped out her pepper spray keychain to blind him. He'd volunteer to be gut shot before ever being sprayed with that evil shit again.

"Oh, am I?" Her belligerent tone was not a surprise. No gun came forth to add meaning to her justified attitude. Reece was glad she wasn't a frail little flower.

He nodded, shaping an innocent smile on his lips. "I'm afraid so."

She stood and put one hand on her hip. "I know you don't know this about me, since we're strangers and all, but I've changed a flat tire before, so you can run along." She glanced back to her task, muttering, "I'm not *either* doing it wrong."

He tilted his head to one side and smiled at her frustrated expression. Crossing his arms, he leaned against the light pole behind him and prepared to watch the show.

Her narrowed gaze pierced his face. "What do you think you're doing?"

"I want to watch and learn, oh great experienced tire changer."

"Why? Need some pointers?" One beautiful brow lifted in challenge.

He laughed. "No. I want to watch and see how you loosen the lug nuts on that flat tire once your car is jacked up all the way in the air. So please, do carry on." He gestured for her to continue.

She turned back to the tire and muttered another whispered curse, "...stupid frickin' lug nuts..." She twisted back with an angry expression, which quickly softened into a heart-melting grin. "Well, I guess you've got me there."

"I'd be happy to help you change that tire. Or ridicule you further while you do it. Lady's choice."

She laughed, picked up the cross-shaped four-way lug wrench, and held it out to him. He leaned up from the post, approached her slowly and took it. He hoped she didn't look down just yet. His cock had reacted fervently and swelled outward another inch in response to the scent of her when he stepped into her personal space to grab the tool. Cursing his self-imposed sexual drought, Reece took a step past her and noticed she let him brush very close without stepping out of the way.

She smelled like sex. Or did everything smell like sex because he wanted her so badly?

"I'll let you get your hands dirty." Her golden blond hair, which brushed her shoulders in curly waves, framed an oval face. Now that he was closer, he saw the color of her eyes. Sea green. Or maybe a color like dew-kissed grass.

I am a total sap. A big, horny, sappy goof.

8

She was interested in him, too. She stared, most particularly at *his* ass when she thought he wasn't looking. He didn't mind. Turnabout was fair play. She was the perfect height. Tall enough that her head would line up with his shoulders if they hugged, short enough to be able to wear spike heels if they ever went dancing.

He squatted down to change her tire and completed the task in record time. All the while he tried to figure out a way to entice her up to his apartment. He lived across the street and just down the block. Reece wasn't usually such a letch with strange women, but she stirred something deeply important within him, something he'd missed.

Plus, she gave him a record-breaking hard-on. After a night of getting fake hit-on for the sole purpose of gaining entrance into his club, Reece was ready for the interest of someone who didn't want anything from him but company or perhaps, better yet, pleasure.

He glanced at his apartment building, wondering what he could say to get her to accompany him inside. His car was parked in a garage a block away. He'd been on his way home after a long night at work when she had distracted him. Her and her shapely, sexy ass. He kicked the release on the jack, lowered the car to the ground, tightened the final lug nut in place on the replacement tire, and stood with the intention of being charming.

"Are you married?" she asked before he could say a word. She stepped directly into his personal space. He inhaled, taking in and memorizing her lovely scent.

"No. Are you?" He breathed in her unique fragrance once more. This time he wasn't as circumspect. The dance of love had begun. She was considering him, he could tell. Otherwise, why would it matter if he had a wife?

"Nope." Her voice lowered to a husky tone with that

single-word answer. She reached out as she spoke and smoothed the front of his jacket with her palm. "I've never even been engaged." The sensation of her touch sent a pulse of desire straight to his balls.

"Good." He was glad he still had the ability to speak without simply grunting a response. He reached up and trapped her hand on his chest, caressing her soft skin with his thumb.

"Is it good?" She took another step closer. Her breasts brushed his upper torso. Her hips rested against his. She couldn't possibly miss his cock trying its best to stand at attention to impress her.

He raised his free hand to tuck a stray lock of her soft hair behind her ear and whispered, "It will be." He genuinely hoped they were having the same conversation. He was talking about sweaty, satisfying sex.

"Do you promise?" Her head tilted, eyes seeking his, and he knew she certainly couldn't miss the beast in his pants throbbing forward in response, promising all good things to come if she'd only accompany him to his apartment.

"I do." Reece used his best convincing voice to add, "I know you don't know this about me, since we're strangers and all, but I—" The sudden connection of her seductive mouth pressing to his cut off whatever he was about to say, which he couldn't remember anyway because her tongue licked his bottom lip and slipped inside to caress gently about.

For his part, he dragged her up into his arms. She slanted her mouth across his to deepen this, their first intoxicating kiss. Perfection.

"Do you live close?" she asked, breaking the luscious connection just long enough to ask the question before planting her mouth on his again. One of her hands slid around to brush the stubble at the nape of his neck. He kept his hair very closely cropped. As a bouncer for a premier club, it completed his dangerous bad-assed look. He was glad she wasn't deterred in any way by his appearance. Some women told him they found him frightening, right before they got a glint in their eye that said they were willing to do *anything* to get inside his club.

He tightened his grasp around her and twisted them until he pressed her against the car. He slid a hand down her back, fingertips feeling their way to cup her lovely ass. He pressed her more firmly into his groin, which was already grinding against her rhythmically. His cock stiffened and pulsed in anticipation, gearing up to do the deed here and now on the street corner.

A glimpse of sanity intruded. Perhaps he shouldn't treat her like a prostitute. She felt incredibly good...but perhaps he should make sure she *wasn't* a prostitute.

He broke from the kiss. "Yes. I live very close. What's your name?"

Her panicked look startled him as her whole body stiffened. "No names!"

"What?"

She took a deep breath, pushed it out slowly, and melted back into him. "No names," she repeated softly. "Can't this just be a private, mutually beneficial evening without an exchange of detailed information?"

"Sure. Okay. No names. How about if I call you Smith? Or did you want to be Jones?" This was an interesting conundrum. The name he would have given her was Mark Reece. It was the undercover name he used for his current job as a bouncer. He wondered what *she* was hiding from.

"Gentleman's choice." She grabbed a handful of his ass and brought him close. "I just want to get naked with you. Is that too bold of me?"

"No. But aren't you worried? I mean, I *am* a stranger

and all." *And I'm scary looking to some women, but not to you, apparently.*

"Are you going to hurt me?" She flashed a grin and he wanted to eat her up one bite at a time.

Amused, he said, "No." He was going to make sweet love to her until they were both sweaty, breathing hard and completely satisfied. "I was about to assure you that I'd never let any harm come to you."

"That's what I thought. Besides, I can take care of myself. Also, I have a good feeling about you, Jones."

"What are you basing your feeling on?" He nudged her with his hips, allowing his cock to introduce itself yet again, like the unruly beast hadn't already been dry humping her for the last several minutes in blatant overture.

"You smell nice, you have a sense of humor, and you did me a huge favor changing that tire. But mostly, I've been a long time without the comfort of a man. I believe you're worth taking a chance on." She nudged back and he had to close his eyes a moment. This whole situation smacked of *setup.*

Then why wasn't he getting that tingly feeling in his belly that things weren't what they seemed?

Maybe she really *was* looking for a quick and easy hookup with no strings attached. He shouldn't let his little head dictate this evening. What was she after? Was this no-names thing a ploy?

"So are you looking for a new boyfriend or a sugar daddy or something and just reeling me in for a later changeup?"

Her eyes widened in surprise. "No. I swear. I'm only looking for an anonymous Mr. Right Now, not a forever commitment. I don't want a permanent fixture in my life, just some sex tonight. Okay?"

"Good enough, Smith. I live across the street." He nodded in the direction of his building.

"Perfect. Let's go, Jones."

Reece couldn't believe his good fortune. He put her tools and flat tire in her trunk as his blood sang with delectable sexual possibilities. Closing the trunk soundly, he grabbed her hand. He couldn't decide what to do with her first. Fuck her in the vestibule of his apartment building before she changed her mind? This from the lusty beast in his pants.

No, not my style. At least find a soft surface. His bed had a very soft surface, and he should taste her first. Tasting her would probably send him over the edge before he even got his cock inside of her body, but what a way to go.

Yes, he would whisk her up to his apartment and taste her first. Always a popular appetizer to make the rest of the night last longer. Besides, he'd been too long without the comfort of a woman to be good enough his first round through.

Being undercover for so long gave him limited options with regard to any sort of love life. This arrangement of two sexually deprived people on a path to an anonymous, lust-filled night of passion worked perfectly if he never wanted to see her again.

Reece inhaled her delectable fragrance once more, glanced at the top of her blonde head and wondered if one night would be enough to quench his already sizable thirst for her.

Jessica was about to get laid. *Hallelujah!* The delicious stranger who had so expertly changed her tire also set off her sexy man pheromone warning system the minute he stepped into sensory range. He was tall and muscular with dark hair and chocolate-brown eyes. He had casual clothing under a nice leather jacket, not like a scruffy biker one. He was a big guy, imposing because of his height, but she didn't feel the least uncomfortable in his presence. He was engaging, mesmerizing, completely unfamiliar and she was falling in lust with him.

She watched his hands as he removed the tire from her car and enviously wished those large, square-shaped fingers caressed her body instead of her steel-belted radial. She wanted him to skip the tire change and work on her. Her head had been filled with questions. Would he have sex with her? Was he the one? Wasn't he already the perfect choice to rid her of her virginal status issues?

As he worked, she developed a plan. If she could talk this delectable stranger into a quick round of take-me-tonight sex, then when she went back to work on Monday, she'd no longer be a virgin.

Neil Wiley wouldn't have any gossip to share about her. Everyone knew she couldn't tell a lie to save her own life. She'd easily be able to say, "Of course I'm not a virgin."

So if Neil tried to embarrass her in front of her co-workers—and he would—she'd be able to laugh it off and say she and Kelli were only joking. She'd tell everyone in range that they'd known Neil listened in on their private conversation and had been winding him up. It would be good to see Neil embarrassed for a change.

Most importantly, they could even strap her to a lie detector and ask her if she'd ever had sex, to which she could answer truthfully, "Of course I have!" *If* and only if she got Mr. Delicious to cooperate with her tonight. Her loathsome virginity could be a part of her past within the next hour if she played her cards right.

She'd stolen that first kiss to make her final decision about this crazy plan, using it as a basis for further action. If he rang her bell with a single kiss—and he had—then she'd follow him to a quiet place and expect that he knew what he was doing sexually. Even if he didn't and he simply removed her virginity with one single thrust instead of climaxing before he ever got inside of her body, she'd be grateful.

Filled with optimistic confidence, she planned to remain in bold mode so the sexy stranger wouldn't know she was a virgin by her wild actions. The more sexually overt she was, the surer she was she could pull this off. In the unlikely event he got out of hand, she could kick his ass. She had training in that arena at least, more than she'd had in the sexual arena, ironically—or maybe sadly—enough.

She locked up her car and breathed a sigh of relief her service weapon was still hidden in the trunk. She'd stowed it there to go out with Kelli tonight. So, if Mr. Delicious ever *didn't* take no for an answer in the coming night, she'd simply kick his ass the old-fashioned way, using her hand-to-hand combat skills.

Jessica had learned quite a lot from four older brothers before she ever joined the FBI. She'd also been top of her class during her field training, likely because of the previous training with her siblings. Jessica didn't expect to need these skills. She had a warm feeling about Jones.

He had a sense of humor, and he'd changed her tire like a knight in shining armor. While she could change a tire as fast as any of her brothers, she usually chose not to. Wisps of her inner girly-girl came out in vehicle-related work projects.

She was very grateful for his assistance in saving her manicure. Plus, he'd been right. She'd been so wound up and angry about Neil listening in to her private conversation with Kelli earlier that she hadn't been paying attention to what she was doing. Normally, of course she'd have loosened the bolts before jacking up the car.

Jones held her hand as they crossed the street and walked half a block or so further to a very nice tall brick apartment building. He put an arm around her and leaned in to kiss her temple before using the code to open the outer door leading inside. Jessica rested her head on his shoulder a moment before they entered. Do or die. This was the moment of no return. He held the door for her and she entered.

They walked arm in arm to the elevator in the empty ground-floor vestibule. Inside, they clung to each other. He punched the eighth-floor button before he turned, pushed his face near and planted his mouth on hers. His tongue stroked inside her mouth deeply and passionately as they ascended. The ding of the elevator announced the opening of the doors. The sound broke the elevator sex fantasy she was having as she wrapped herself around his body seductively and pressed him into the corner of the small space.

He held her close, stepped into the hallway and said, "I want you to understand one thing before we enter my apartment." He paused. "I'll never get a housekeeper of the year award." She laughed because she'd been expecting him to say something honorable about his intentions once they crossed the threshold of his domain.

He smiled wolfishly, negating any fear of honorable intentions as he approached a door on the right. He unlocked it with a key from his front pocket. She couldn't help but notice his erection hadn't subsided and smiled inwardly. He ushered her inside a fairly neat space. It had bachelor written all over it, but it didn't matter because she wasn't here for the decor.

"Listen, Smith. One other thing I want you to know is—"

"That you don't usually do this. Yeah, me either, but

you are simply irresistible." Jessica stepped closer and inhaled deeply. The smell of him calmed her at the same time it sent zinging snaps of arousal to every erogenous zone she possessed.

He laughed. "I rarely have beautiful women proposition me. Except at where I work and you should know that I always turn work-related offers down. I'm glad I excluded you from my turn-down pile tonight." He reached out to touch her face.

She stepped back, resolutely avoiding his caress. "No names, no job descriptions. I need this to be anonymous, or I'm out of here and headed back to my car with the newly changed tire, thank you very much."

He put both hands up in surrender. "I get it. Anonymous. No worries." He moved back in, all sexy man and dangerous looks. His large, talented hands wrapped around either side of her waist. But he just stared at her.

She threw her arms around his neck and kissed him to get things going. The mechanics, she understood, but not the seduction along the way. Her experience was severely lacking in many areas beyond the physical act itself, she decided quickly. She hoped Jones would not require her to know too much because she *didn't* know much. Except that he sincerely made her want to peel her clothes off and dance naked.

Jones wrapped his strong arms around her, then slid his mouth over hers, hypnotically stroking his tongue through her lips and over every surface inside her mouth as if cataloging the interior for future reference.

He slipped a hand down to her ass, cupped one cheek and pulled her closer to the very impressive bulge in his pants. She pushed a hand down between them to stroke the front of his jeans to determine if he stuffed anything down his boxers to make himself look bigger.

Jones felt humongous against her belly.

He growled when she grabbed his cock and squeezed, discovering it was *all* him with no sock filler whatsoever. Excellent. Jones had absolutely nothing to be ashamed of in whatever locker rooms he frequented and this would be great for her.

One small, panicked thought registered. In order to accomplish her goal, his large cock was going to have to fit inside her virgin territory...some way, some how. Perhaps that would work in her favor to keep him from realizing she was untried in this arena. As big as he was, surly most women were a tight fit.

The thought simultaneously thrilled and concerned her, but she wanted him. The sexual vision of coupling with him sent a rush of moisture into her panties, making her shiver in delight.

Jones absorbed her trembling and danced them still kissing, stroking and clinging to each other across the floor towards an open door. She hesitated at the entryway of the dark room and broke the sultry, tonsil-licking kiss to contemplate what she was about to *finally* carry out.

Do or die, now or never, this she knew was her absolute final chance to stop and reconsider.

"Smith?" he whispered, leaning down to kiss her collarbone. "Having second thoughts?"

"Maybe," she said, gazing at his fine body and handsome face.

His lust-filled expression shifted to hers with concern, then softened. "Anything I can do to put your fears to rest and convince you to proceed?"

She looked into his very intent gaze. "Tell me again that you won't expect this to continue after tonight."

He cleared his throat. "What if we're so good together *you* want to continue, Smith? Don't you want to leave your options open?" His lips brushed her temple.

"No. I don't. No options. No names. No job

descriptions. Just an anonymous one-night stand to scratch an aggressive itch. Promise me that's all this is for you."

Jones leaned in closer. His breath caressed her ear when he said, "I won't expect this to continue. I'll be grateful to get my itch scratched, I promise."

"Okay then." Jessica took a giant mental step and crossed the boundary to her untried wicked side. She allowed him to lead her by the hand into his bedroom.

The space was large, as was the bed, which was made up neatly despite his warning about the lack of housekeeping. It was a foolish reason to relax her guard, but she did. He left her to turn on a lamp by the bed. He pulled the covers halfway down to expose the sheets. Low light filtered through the shade as he turned and approached her again.

Her apprehension had to be visible as she fought with the last vestiges of her overprotective conscious regarding her imminent actions. She was going to get laid. *Finally*. She kicked her good intentions to the curb and placed her hands at his waist to draw him closer for another kiss.

Slowly they undressed each other, kissing passionately as each article of clothing was removed and dropped to the floor. Once she was down to her bra and panties her desire to get on with this act increased tenfold. It was going to happen. She was going to have sex. She suppressed the urge to squeal like a teen girl at a boy band concert.

Jones leaned down to slide his jeans off his legs and kissed her belly near the skimpy line of her panties. And then he did it again while removing his underwear. A totally naked and very aroused man stood before her.

She noted the unbound size of his cock now fully engorged and ready to play, with her, on this momentous night. She shivered again in anticipation.

Tonight she would lose her annoying virginity to a gorgeous, delicious and very well-hung stranger. Fabulous fate had smiled on her after all.

Without warning, Jones dropped to his knees and planted a juicy kiss below her navel. His mouth trailed downward until she felt him lick her through her moistened panties. She sucked in a surprised breath and uttered a small scream of excitement.

Was she truly really ready for this?

CHAPTER 2

"What are you doing?"

Her panicked tone surprised him.

Reece stopped. He'd shucked off his pants and boxers and knelt before her to pull her sexy little panties off with his teeth. He licked her once, guessing at the location of her clit. By the way she jumped and shrieked, he thought he'd hit it dead on.

"Undressing you." He hooked two fingers in the string bikini panties at the sides of her hips. He slowly pulled her underwear down, revealing she was a natural blonde and that she smelled fantastic. He leaned in for another lick now that she was displayed before him and he definitely hit the target this time.

"Oh!" She moved back half a step, but her hands went to his head as if to steady herself. "I didn't expect..."

Reece looked up her gorgeous body at her lust-glazed eyes. "The thing is, Smith, it's been a long time since any woman has talked me into this, so I'm ashamed to say I'm pretty sure I'm going to last about three strokes before I climax the first time. That is if I don't come on your leg after fully tasting you. But I promise the second time I'll last much longer."

"The second time?"

He sent her a grin. "Yeah."

She exhaled and nodded. "Okay."

"And the third time will be even longer than the second."

"Three times?" she scoffed. "Now you're just bragging."

He laughed. "You'll see." He stood and pushed her gently towards his bed. He popped open the front enclosure of her bra, which seemed to startle her. He peeled it off and promptly licked one peach-colored nipple, the taste of which delighted him.

She inhaled deeply and her hands landed on his shoulders. Her nails pierced his skin deliciously as he ran his thumb across the other nipple while he suckled her. He released the first delectable peak and kissed his way between her breasts to capture the other one for a taste.

Her breathy little cries of pleasure were seriously making him anxious to move things along. He sensed that Smith was skittish. It was likely her first time with a stranger, even though she exuded pure bravado. For his own capabilities, Reece needed to slow things down for their first time together. He pressed on her shoulders until she sat on the edge of the bed, then spread her knees apart and knelt before her again.

Putting a hand under each thigh, he leaned in and pushed his face between her legs to get a better taste of the candy he'd sampled before. Her response to his tongue was an inarticulate noise of pleasure, which made his balls tighten. God in heaven, she tasted good. She eased her upper body back slowly onto the bed, giving him better access.

He licked her once more then planted his mouth below, sucking her nub between his lips. Miss Smith was very responsive. She moaned and writhed with every stroke of his tongue. Her fingertips grazed the back of his head, pulling him closer. He slid two fingers into her tight, slick passage as his other hand found and cupped her breast, his fingertips brushing back and forth over her hardened nipple.

She inhaled in another deep lungful of air and held it before arching her back, finally emitting a breathy little scream that made his cock throb. Her vaginal muscles clamped down hard on his fingers. Her breath came in excited little pants of air as she pulled his head away from her delicious dampened mound.

Satisfied in the knowledge she was also satisfied, he kissed her inner thigh and looked up her body, watching her chest rise and fall. Soon she released her breath on a long whimpering sigh. She was so beautiful.

Reece kissed his way across her belly. He climbed up on all fours on the bed over her and clamped his mouth down on the center of one perfect breast.

Soon her fingers found their way to his face. He kissed a path to her throat and whispered, "You taste like candy."

She laughed lightly and kissed his cheek. "Oh, Jones, you sure know how to get a girl's attention, but I'm ready for those three strokes you promised me."

"Well, then, let me ready myself to plunder you, Miss Smith." He leaned up onto his knees and grabbed a condom from his bedside supply, securing it carefully before turning back to her.

"Any position you had in mind, Smith? Now is the time for requests."

"Gentleman's choice, Jones. You earned it." She sighed as if in contentment. Good.

He decided to keep things simple and go missionary. From the brief exploration with his fingers, he could tell she was snug. Besides, on top he could thrust better. He grabbed his latex covered cock and directed it to her drenched opening, sliding it across her clit a time or two to gather a little moisture before inserting the tip an inch or so inside. *It was utter paradise.*

He concentrated on her face, wanting to watch her expression as he slid inside her for the first time. Shit, he might not even make it three strokes. He might blow apart with his first stroke inside her excruciatingly tight, sexy body. Especially if she watched him as she did now...with wonder for what was sure to be a very disappointing, short-lived experience. But he planned to make it up to her the second time. Hopefully, there would be a second time.

Her eyes widened as his cock slid inside that first inch. The nirvana-inducing feeling of her body around that barest part of him made his eyes lower halfway in bliss. Damn, she was tight.

"Harder, Jones. I like it hard," she whispered and pulled his head down for a kiss.

She licked his lips, but he wanted to watch her, so he pulled back and thrust deeply inside, hard like she'd asked him to. Her eyes closed and her head dipped back as he filled her up. She sucked in a deep sexy breath. Her fingers, resting on his biceps, dug into his skin the moment he stopped moving forward.

Fully impaled to his balls, he took a deep breath to stop from losing it with a single stroke. She was more than tight, like a luscious vise on his grateful cock. He centered himself, withdrew halfway and sank into her slick warmth again, and again, and again.

She whimpered and the sound of her little cries as he stroked drove him insane with the need to release. One of her legs slipped around the back of his thigh and rubbed up and down. With the next thrust she lifted her hips and ground into him to meet his push inside. He couldn't believe he hadn't climaxed yet. He was on the edge of it. He wanted it. He stroked within her faster, harder, longer than he thought he could possibly last given her snug capacity.

All of a sudden, she stiffened in his arms and cried out. Her internal muscles clamped down on his sensitive cock in yet another release. Her unexpected climax sent his libido into overdrive. Pleasure ripped through his lower half. He sped his thrusts in anticipation of coming at long last.

Reece growled as he climaxed, slamming his cock inside her all the way over and over again. His orgasm was wrenched from him in glorious mind-numbing waves. He froze above her for a split second before collapsing in a gratified if undignified heap, still deeply embedded inside her, trying to catch his breath from the best fucking sex he'd had since, well, ever.

His body covered her slighter one completely. Her breath came in short gasps and tickled his ear. Soon she ran her fingernails up and down his spine, lightly rasping his back.

"That was more than three strokes, Jones." He heard the amusement in her tone.

"Was it? Sorry, Smith, I never was any good at math."

"I forgive you, but I can't breathe."

He rose to his forearms, lifting his torso off of her, still feeling like his body had turned to honey. "Better?"

"Yes. Thank you, Jones. Amazing scratching, by the way."

"You too, Smith. My eagerness is slightly abated, for now." He leaned down and kissed her lips tenderly. "I'll be right back."

He slid out of her and got up. Walking on shaky legs to the bathroom, he wondered if this one-night stand with the anonymous Miss Smith was going to be enough for him. He already wanted her again and the lusty beast between his legs did, too. It was a bad idea to develop feelings for this beautiful surprise guest, especially in his line of work, but he found it difficult not to briefly fantasize about it anyway.

Jessica had always hoped her first sexual interlude would be worth the effort. Whew. Was it ever! She'd made a good choice with Jones. He knew things. Good things. Decadent things. Body-rocking, orgasmic things.

She heard water running and wondered if she had time to slip out of his apartment before he returned. But then she remembered his promise of a second and a third time and decided she could stay for a couple more rounds with the very delectable Mr. Jones and his magical lips and fingers. There was also his impressive cock to look forward to.

When he'd thrust in the first time to the hilt, she felt a slight tearing inside, but he was so big, she didn't feel anything else except his huge size after the first hint of pain. Thank heavens. Having him fill her to the brink was undeniably the most amazing experience she'd ever had. Way better than she'd expected, and best of all she wasn't a virgin anymore. Plus, he'd given her orgasms. Two of them!

The door to his bathroom opened and even in the low light she could see his relieved expression when he saw her waiting in the bed. She was glad she hadn't sneaked out just yet. One more time with him and then she'd leave.

"Glad you stuck around, Miss Smith." Mr. Delicious crossed the room to the bed.

"Me too, Mr. Jones. What else do you have in store for me tonight?"

"Whatever your heart desires." He slid under the sheets on his side. With one hand propping up his head as the glow from the lamp caressed his face, he grinned as if anticipating their next round of sexual pleasure.

She inhaled. The air around them smelled like sex. She finally understood that phrase. The scent was musky and tangy yet delectable, a fragrance very hard to define, but the exotic aroma made her want more of it.

"Kiss me again, Jones. You're very good at it. A man who knows how to kiss a woman right is a rare find."

"Really? Why, thank you, Miss Smith. I'm happy to oblige." He leaned in and kissed her lips with tender attention. One hand came to her face. His thumb stroked her jaw and he kissed her gently, passionately. Her mouth opened to allow his entrance, but he was content to nibble on her lips before licking his way inside for more. Before long his arm slid underneath her head so she could use it for a pillow as his lips caressed hers.

Minutes later his fingertips stroked up and then down her body and she felt him grow steadily against her thigh. She guessed it was time for round two and her body ignited as licks of sensation zipped around her aroused limbs in contemplation of more bliss from Jones and his magic hands.

Her flat tire fiasco would now be a fate-filled memory of her exquisite inaugural sexual experience.

Jones kissed her as his hand wandered across her skin, ultimately slipping between her legs. Amazing how he could find her hottest spot without looking. He stroked her once and she almost bit his tongue. While her itch had been scratched, twice, she found she wanted more. She should take advantage of this one night, and especially this impressive man, while she had the chance.

She reached between them to stroke Jones and his impressive cock, eliciting a groan of pleasure. Leaning forward, brushing his chest over her sensitive nipples, he grabbed another condom from the nightstand. She took it from him and put it on herself this time. Obviously another first for her, but he didn't seem to notice. He took shallow breaths and gave her a glazed, lust-filled stare as she rolled the latex slowly and carefully over his huge cock, her fingertips brushing the neatly trimmed nest of dark curly hair at the base. Sexy.

Once her task was complete she moved to her side again so that they faced each other. He slipped an arm around her and his fingertips caressed her lower back. He stroked one cheek of her butt as he watched her. Pulling her leg up over his hip, Jones snuggled closer until his cock rested at the apex of her thighs.

He kissed her tenderly, nibbling from one corner of her mouth to the other. His cock nudged between her legs until it rested against her intimately, stroking across her hot spot several times until her breaths became gasps.

With careful precision, he inched himself between her slick inner walls until he was fully seated. She sighed in contentment. He stopped and held her close, all the while kissing her more tenderly than she'd ever been kissed in her life.

The whole experience was seductive in its intensity. It moved her. She'd never felt so deeply connected to anyone. No pun intended, she just felt so good. He stroked her body as if he'd memorized the map of her skin and applied all his expertise to the sexual experience they shared.

His hand massaged down her spine until it found the dimples at the base. With hypnotic slowness he pulled halfway out, only to enter her again at the same speed. She could feel his hand at the base of her spine as if holding her in place to slowly seduce and plunder her decadently.

As the rhythm of his strokes began to increase, she felt his fingertips skim to the peak of one breast. He stroked her nipple, which pebbled against his hand. He pinched the tip delicately between finger and thumb, sending spiraling sensations rippling down her body to where they joined together.

Jessica thrust her hips forward in response, meeting him halfway for each stroke, which stretched her deliciously. She was building to another explosive climax.

His hand dipped from her breast to slide between her legs. He broke the kiss and leaned back to study her face. He stroked her with his fingers once, forcing a moan as her eyes closed in sublime pleasure, waiting for more.

"Open your eyes, Smith. I want to watch you climax this time."

"Oh." Her eyes popped open.

He stroked her in reward, increasing the speed and pressure as his erotic gaze warmed her. All the while he slid himself in and out of her body at a steady pace until a flash of arousal inside her built to a crescendo of the ultimate pleasure.

She gasped but couldn't keep her eyes open when the orgasm washed over her in waves of luscious gratification. Her internal muscles clamped down on him repeatedly as he rocked in and out of her body, over and over.

He made a satisfied groan when she opened her eyes to meet his. His hand slid to her ass and she pushed forward as the speed of his thrusts increased. She watched his face. His eyes slid half shut and opened again.

"I want to watch you come too, Jones," she said.

He flashed her a devilish smile as his stare devoured her heart and soul. "As you wish." He stroked deeply inside one more time and groaned. His head tilted back slightly and his spine arched in what looked like pleasure or pain. Maybe both.

After several moments of heavy breathing on both their parts, Jones took a deep breath and pierced her with a seductive stare. "You're amazing, Miss Smith. Simply amazing." He leaned forward and captured her lips in another long, tender kiss.

With round two complete, her sated body relaxed against his sheets. He kissed her face a few times before he withdrew to the bathroom. She should leave, but decided to just close her eyes for a couple of minutes first and relax. She was already half-dozing when he returned and pressed soft kisses to her face, neck and mouth.

Jessica woke sometime in the middle of the night in a strange bed. A masculine arm was wrapped around her shoulder and for a second she couldn't remember how on earth it got there. The memories of her past several hours soon danced into her sexually satisfied brain. Mr. Delicious, aka Mr. Jones, had rocked her world. Repeatedly.

Good Lord, he was fabulous. After a short nap, Jessica had crawled on top of him for the promised third round. She wanted to try out a more aggressive coupling where she was in charge. He didn't seem to mind and in fact encouraged her to ride him rather enthusiastically.

She fell asleep directly after round three on top of his chest. Later, she'd woken with him spooned behind her. She thought about trying to slip away without disturbing him, but instead wanted to kiss him one last time. He woke up and talked her into round four.

"Just one more time, Smith," he'd coaxed, stroking her in places he'd learned she responded to. He was just so good she couldn't turn him down. He moved on top of her, taking his time making love to her slowly and lasting longer than any of the previous rounds. After a fifth shattering climax, she'd slept hard.

Jessica glanced at the bedside clock, and then did a

double take because she couldn't believe the time. It would be dawn soon. It was well past time for her to leave. The longer she stayed, the more worried she became that he'd learn her identity. She wanted to sneak out. If he woke up, she knew they'd be rolling around on his silky sheets once again. Not exactly a detriment, but it was well past time to go. Four rounds on her first night, including five orgasms, certainly qualified as getting her proverbial money's worth.

Jessica pondered leaving him a note—she felt a bit guilty at the thought of just walking away after such an important night—but what could she say? Thanks for being my first? Best first sex ever? No. Better to leave nothing than utter either of those true statements.

She lifted his muscular arm from her body and slid out of his bed and onto the floor. He didn't move a muscle, sleeping as hard as she had earlier. Jessica gathered her clothing in the dark and dressed in his living room. She glanced around for a pen and piece of paper. The sound of him stirring in bed made her give up any thoughts of leaving a note. She scooted out of his apartment, down the elevator and out the building's front door.

The gray of night diminished and dawn's light seeped around the edges of the surrounding buildings. Jessica stretched and repeated to herself, *I'm not a virgin anymore.* She was tired from lack of sleep, had used muscles she didn't even know existed all night long, but felt so incredibly good it was difficult not to grin like a maniac.

Stepping off the curb, she headed toward her car. Not surprisingly, there was no traffic this early on a Sunday morning.

As she crossed the street, the hair on the back of her neck lifted. The sensation of being watched infiltrated her mind and she twisted to look up at his window. Was he watching her run from him? The window she thought was his didn't have a sexy naked man staring out at her, unfortunately. Why was she disappointed? She'd been the one to set the parameters of secrecy regarding their tryst. So how could she already miss a man she'd never see again?

Jones had been right. She should have left her options open. None of the adjacent windows had anyone naked or otherwise looking out at her, so she shook off her foolish fears and quickly made her way to her car.

As she drove away, images of the night before floated around like a misty dream in her satisfied mind. A smile crept up and then a giggle escaped. Jessica Hayes, FBI agent, had just spent the night with a delectable stranger for her first sexual experience ever.

She couldn't wait to tell Kelli tomorrow when they met at the new coffee shop near Kelli's office. The subject of discussion would now be her *former* virginal status issue, which made her grin even wider. She flipped on the radio and sang along to every song as the eastern skyline began to brighten into early morning.

Jessica's only regret was insisting on fake names. Then again, she *did* know where he lived. Perhaps she'd surprise him one day.

CHAPTER 3

Jessica started Monday with an extra bounce in her step. She hadn't stopped smiling in more than twenty-four hours. Even facing Neil Wiley, smarmy bane of her existence, didn't worry her as she got ready for work.

Perhaps she'd go down to the HR department and file a complaint if Neil ever said another word to her. Probably she should have reported him earlier. She'd deemed this course of action a last resort, and one she'd never seriously considered until this past weekend. He was very well connected. Jessica always pictured that his nepotism would win all battles if she went up against him even using HR.

But she felt braver in light of her recent accomplishment. Maybe losing her virginity had strengthened her backbone. Her mind slipped easily down memory lane as poignant moments of her time with Jones seeped in.

A pang of regret—not the first—crossed her mind, but she batted it down. Jones would forever live in a special place in her heart as her fabulous first lover. She left her place and started for her car. More flashes of their erotic night intruded and her stride hitched at the intensity of the remembered sensation of his hands and mouth on her, stroking her heated flesh.

The explosion of her climax reverberated through her memory. The regret accumulated as she wondered how she would find another man who was as good a lover as Jones. Strictly speaking, she didn't have to search very hard. She had some contacts in her line of work, and she *did* have his address. If she ever decided to pursue him, she could find out exactly who Mr. Jones really was.

She shook off her heated reverie to examine later and slid into her car. A mental voice noted that the coffee shop where she was meeting Kelli was near the bar *and* the apartment of one delicious Mr. Jones. Stop it. No driving by his street. She was the one who insisted on anonymity. Besides, she'd slipped away without saying goodbye or thank you or "do me Jonesy one more time." *Nothing.*

If a guy had done that, he'd be vilified. She rolled her eyes at her clichéd double-standard behavior. In retrospect, Jessica should have at the very least left a note of sincere thanks, or indulged in one last kiss before slinking out of his apartment at dawn like she'd done something wrong. When in fact there had been four amazing rounds of right that had taken place there.

If she hadn't been afraid he'd wake up and seduce her into round five, she might have taken one last taste of his luscious lips. Which was how round four had come about in the wee hours of the morning. She'd rolled out from under his arm, sat up and been ready to go when the compulsion to kiss his mouth one last time came over her.

His wonderful lips had teased and tortured, licked and kissed and she'd nearly begged him to take her by the time he got around to entering her tender body that last time. But she'd been wet and ready for him. She clung to him, reveled in the sensations he evoked, caressed his muscular form as he slowly made love to her, sweetly touching her soul with that final shuddering, unexpectedly soul-wrenching climax. *Sigh.*

She parked her car in the coffee shop's small lot, got out and walked around the rear bumper. Her eye fell on the donut spare tire. It spurred a flashback of round three, when she'd been on top, and she almost stumbled in her tracks. This was ridiculous. All that from seeing a tire? She had to get a grip. It was time to focus on her Monday morning. She noticed Kelli's neon yellow Volkswagen bug already in the parking lot.

Jessica couldn't wait to share her great news.

Shaking off her sexy memories with difficulty, Jessica marched toward the entry. An uneasy sensation stirred in her stomach as she approached. This coffee shop was a little off the beaten path, but it seemed too quiet for a Monday morning. Her bad feeling didn't abate as she advanced on the glass front door. Her steps slowed.

Through the glass, she could see the six-foot divider topped by fake foliage that separated the tiny entryway from the rest of the shop. She couldn't see inside, but neither could anyone inside see out the door.

The closed sign was flipped outward, but the door was slightly ajar. Her professional instincts screaming, Jessica pushed it open silently. The deadbolt lock protruded out of the metal side, as if the door hadn't closed completely before the lock was snapped. Why would the door be locked? Something was wrong.

She opened the door just wide enough to slip inside, then closed it quietly behind her and waited. She thought she heard the stifled sound of crying. Moving as softly as she could, she walked along the divider toward the main area of the coffee shop.

The hair on the back of her neck that had been prickling stood straight on end when she heard several screams. The sounds of chairs scraping came next.

"Anyone makes a move, and I blow her head off!" said an unseen angry male voice.

Jessica reached under her jacket and fingered the shoulder holster of her service weapon. She should exit and call for backup, but the unseen gunman drifted into her vision before she could leave. He wore a black ski mask and had his arm slung around Kelli's neck. He waved a gun towards the rest of the room, then put it back at Kelli's temple.

If he turned to look at the front door, he would see her. Jessica drew her weapon slowly and flipped off the safety as she focused on Kelli. She crouched next to the divider. The look of pure terror on Kelli's face made Jessica's rash intent more palpable.

In an instant, the gunman turned toward the door. She had only a second to react before he registered her crouched there.

"FBI! Drop your weapon!" she shouted.

The gunman automatically turned his gun towards Jessica, inadvertently twisting Kelli out of the way as he did so. He raised his arm, took quick aim and leveled his pistol as if ready to fire. So Jessica shot him in the leg. He cried out and dropped to the floor. Released, Kelli stumbled clear. Jessica leapt up and kept her gun on him. She ducked her head past the divider and back, praying there was only one gunman. Her quick survey registered a blur of non-threatening faces, no ski masks. Seeing Kelli was safely out of reach, Jessica quickly stepped to the man writhing on the floor screaming and kicked his pistol away from his body.

She took another step to the left and into the main area of the coffee shop to assess further threat potential. The 9mm Beretta clutched in her hands was pointed slightly down at the floor. No need to accidentally shoot a patron. She noted only a few customers with hands in the air. She relaxed and turned back to a tearful Kelli.

Kelli tried to speak, but couldn't. Something still wasn't right. Jessica realized, too late, the gunman she'd shot was not alone.

The second man came up from behind the counter where the register was. As though in slow motion, she saw the sinister expression in his eyes through the slit in the black ski mask as he leveled a gun in her direction.

He pulled the trigger. She'd failed to secure the area before relaxing her guard and now she'd pay for her incompetence with her life. This would teach her to charge in unprepared without backup.

She froze, tensing in anticipation of getting shot. The strong-armed shove to her shoulder probably saved her life. She sucked in a surprised breath at the contact and fell to one knee in an unbalanced heap. The bullet whizzed past her head but she brought her gun up, aimed at the scumbag who'd just shot at her.

"Drop it!"

"Fuck off, bitch," he responded.

She shot him in the hand before he could take another shot at her. The money the shooter had been grabbing from the cash register flew into the air as he dropped his gun to hold his wounded, bleeding hand. Jessica heard the wail of sirens approaching faintly as if from a long distance.

The guy she'd shot in the leg wasn't going anywhere. Jessica stood and approached the man behind the counter, pulling handcuffs out of her purse one-handed. It still miraculously hung on her shoulder.

"You shot me, you fucking bitch!" The gunman held his bleeding wound as if he couldn't believe she'd defended herself.

"Yeah? Well, you shot at me first." She forced him to lie facedown on the floor and kept her gun pointed at his head until she could get his good hand cuffed to a metal rack behind the counter. It held neat little rows of coffee packages, but if he tried to get away it would make a lot of noise and slow him down.

She moved to the end of the counter, where she could keep an eye on both ski-masked men. The police arrived and entered, guns drawn.

"Drop your weapon!"

"I'm an FBI special agent," she said non-threateningly. She placed her weapon on the floor at her feet, knowing she'd have to surrender it to an evidence bag. She stuck her hands in the air and backed up a step. She now had her back to all the other patrons. "There's the guy by the door and one secured behind the counter here with my handcuffs."

Kelli stood over the whimpering first gunman. A police officer squatted over him, checked him and used his com to call for an ambulance. All Jessica could think of was the mountains of paperwork she'd have to fill out for this escapade today. And she hadn't even had any caffeine yet.

"Where's your ID?" the officer asked as he kicked her gun to the side.

"In my front pocket."

"Got any other weapons on your person?"

"Yes." She sighed. "I have an ankle holster, and a knife." This was not the way to start out a Monday morning, especially not after such a memorable Saturday night with Mr. Delicious. She still had to tell Kelli about the fabulous sex she'd shared with an anonymous stranger. *After* she got a cup of coffee.

The officer kept his gun on her. "Reach slowly into your pocket and get your ID."

Jessica pulled out her badge with two fingers. She palmed it and flipped it open one-handed.

The officer studied it a moment and then lowered his weapon. "Sorry. We have to check everyone out."

"I know."

The officer glanced down at her weapon on the floor. "Also, you'll have to surrender the weapon you fired for evidence."

"I know that, too." She wasn't upset. That was protocol. At least another gun would be brought to her before she left the scene. She gave him a small smile of assurance and turned as Kelli approached with a slightly shell-shocked expression.

"Are you okay?" Jessica hugged Kelli to her a moment. The police were milling around, checking things out and talking to the scared and relieved patrons.

"You sure do know how to make an entrance, Jessica."

"I try."

"Now that you've finished shooting all the bad guys, I have good news for you."

"I have news too—"

"I found someone to help you with your problem." Her gaze shifted over Jessica's left shoulder. Jessica felt someone approach from behind and a recently familiar scent wafted around her. Sex. Man. Mr. Delicious. Jones?

Kelli's words didn't register. Problem? What problem? She turned to see the person Kelli was staring at.

Oh no. Shit. Shit. Shit.

The only man in the world with intimate carnal knowledge of her body stared back at her. Jones stood a pace away, a slightly sardonic smile on his face.

"Mark Reece, this is Jessica Hayes. She's the one I told you about," Kelli said in a voice Jessica considered very loud.

No. No. No. This could not be happening. Kelli had told Mr. Delicious she needed to be deflowered?

Kill me. Kill me now.

"Hi, Jessica Hayes," he said in a sultry, sexy, now-I-know-your-name tone of voice. "I'm very pleased to meet you."

He extended his hand. A hand she remembered vividly had brought her to repeated climaxes less than thirty-six hours ago. She reflexively placed her hand in his and he held it longer than he should have for a casual first-time greeting.

The mental image of his large, warm hand snug between her legs, stroking her, intruded and she let go as if he'd burned her. She knew without a doubt as the heat blazed a path across her cheeks that her color was way up.

"Jessica is the one who needs to get laid," Kelli said in a conspiratorial whisper. "And she's never done it before."

"Hasn't she?" Mark winked at Jessica.

"Yes. So don't forget to be gentle with her."

More blood rushed to Jessica's cheeks in mortification. The pressure of her embarrassment was about to start leaking right out of her face.

She tried to keep from shouting in frustration when she said, "Kelli, it's Monday morning and I haven't had coffee yet. You just watched me shoot two people. I had to surrender my weapon, but I have a backup. Say another word on this topic and you're my third target."

Kelli, in her zeal to "help" out, hurriedly said, "Don't worry. Mark's a good guy. He'll treat you right. I promise."

"Great." Jessica put a hand over her eyes and hung her head, wondering what to do. She didn't know what to say to either of them. Kelli, who always ran at the mouth, needed to stop talking. Jones, who in the light of day was even more delicious than she remembered, probably thought she was pathetic.

"Could you give us a minute, Kelli?" the very delicious Jones asked. He took Jessica's arm lightly yet firmly and led her a few feet away to relative peace and quiet in an alcove near the restroom hallway.

"You, *Miss Smith*, have some explaining to do."

"I do not!" she whispered hotly. She tugged her arm away from his hand.

His eyebrows rose. "Those stains on my sheets have a whole new meaning this morning."

"Oh my good heavens. Please stop talking!" She put both of her hands to her face, certain it was about to burst from humiliation with all the blood rushing there.

"Why? Are you going to shoot me, too?"

She dropped her hands and looked at him. His expression was slightly contrite.

"No," she said on a sigh. "It's too much damn paperwork." She gestured to the room at the police officers, paramedics dealing with the wounded suspects and the scared patrons. "And you can see I have a full day's worth ahead of me."

"Are you okay?"

"No! I'm mortified." She looked in Kelli's direction, trying not to send a melting glare, knowing also that her friend just wanted to be helpful.

"Don't be. And besides, that's not what I meant."

She searched his eyes. They held a measure of regret. With his new knowledge, he probably wondered if he'd hurt her Saturday night. It wasn't fair to him not to explain her motives. Especially since Kelli had certainly told him all kinds of intimate things about her already.

She pierced him with a steady gaze. "I just wanted it to be over, you know? I wanted it to be anonymous and over with, and *not* public information."

"Well, lucky for you I hadn't given Kelli my answer—which was no, by the way—to her request to, as she put it, 'gently ease her untried friend into the carnal pleasures of sex,' when the two gunmen arrived."

Jessica winced. She could practically hear Kelli's

voice putting the proposition to him. "Why is that lucky?" Not sure she wanted to hear the answer.

"Well, when I turned her request down—and I was about to—she probably would have asked my friend Mike." He nodded in the direction of a very attractive blond man Kelli was conversing with. "He might have said yes."

"Oh my good heavens. Just take my gun and shoot me." She lowered her gaze to the tiles beneath her feet and put her hand on the gun holster under her jacket, finding it empty. *Shit. Shit. Shit.*

"No thanks. I hear the paperwork really sucks. Besides, your secret is safe with me, Smith. I swear to you."

Jessica shivered at his use of her Saturday night nickname. "Thank you, Jones. I do appreciate it."

The seriousness in his teasing tone calmed her. He *was* a good guy. He wasn't about to rat her out to the world. She took a deep breath. Let it out slowly. "Thanks for Saturday night, too. It was remarkable, amazing. Words can't really describe it." She directed her look to the floor again, fearful everyone in the room would know her recent carnal history if they so much as looked in her direction.

"For me, too. Shocked the shit out of me when I realized the girl Kelli was talking about a few minutes ago was you."

Her head lifted to send another gaze his way. "Yeah?"

"I see now why you weren't afraid of going off with a stranger. Nice shooting, Miss Smith." His gaze wandered over to the two men she'd shot upon her arrival.

She laughed. "And don't you forget it."

"I won't." He drilled a seductive gaze at her face as if to memorize it. "Not ever."

She didn't think he was talking about her marksmanship.

"Me either," she whispered.

He took a step closer to her. His spicy cologne assailed her senses. She licked her lips. "Are you tender?" His tone had shifted to unease.

His concern was impossible to miss. Perhaps he was worried about the repeated rounds of lovemaking, now that he knew it had been her first time.

"I ache, but not in a bad way. You didn't hurt me, Jones. I promise."

"Good." This time, the smile he gave her made her feel like he was visualizing her naked. Time to break his focus.

"Why were you going to turn Kelli down in her insidious and very loud public quest to get me laid for the first time?"

"I don't let myself out to deflower virgins, as a rule."

"Perhaps you should. You're really good at it."

"Thanks, I think." He laughed suddenly, then his eyes narrowed in speculation. "Would you consider this meeting fate, Smith?"

"What?"

He shrugged. "You know, us seeing each other like this again so soon after...blissful perfection? When I woke up alone, I never expected to see you again. But I wanted to. Maybe you should reconsider your options on further carnal encounters with me. Because I'm most assuredly game, if you're interested."

"No. Thank you." At his obvious disappointment, she rushed to explain. "It's nothing personal, Jones. I just wanted that aspect of my life to be done. And now it is. I need to move on. I'm *not* in the market for a boyfriend. I'm busy building my career. There's not any time in my routine for a regular love life, you know?"

He nodded. "Well, if you ever change your mind, you know where I live."

"Nice to know, Jones. I'm going to tell Kelli that I had sex with a stranger Saturday night. She is never going to know that stranger is you, right?"

"I never kiss and tell, Miss Smith." His lips made her long for a kiss. Jones was an exceptional kisser, tender and thorough, and watching his lush mouth form words right this moment made her shiver.

"Good. Thank you." She looked at his mouth again. With her Monday starting out as it had, Jessica desperately wanted a taste of him to balance things out. Just a small little kiss. She couldn't help but lean closer. Her head tilted back, getting into position to taste him. Just once more.

"Agent Hayes?" The police officer in charge approached her and Jones. "Are you ready to give a statement?"

"Yes," she said, too loud and too fast. Jessica was stunned to realize she'd almost kissed Jones in public. Thankfully, he faded quickly into the crowd of other patrons giving statements to various law enforcement guys stationed around the room.

Jessica inhaled deeply, taking in the smell of strong coffee and sexy man. Fate. She didn't believe in it. But she'd be lying to herself if she didn't admit she'd craved his kiss moments ago.

The officer took her statement. "There's someone from the Federal Building on the way here with a replacement weapon for you."

"Thanks." Her cell phone buzzed in her pocket. She glanced at her watch and realized she was late for work. The read out told her the call was from her boss. Her life intruded on dream-filled things she couldn't have anyway.

She answered, "Agent Hayes."

Special Agent-in-Charge Butch Martin asked, "Where are you, Hayes?" She suspected he'd already been notified, especially if the Bureau had sent someone with a replacement gun.

"I interrupted an armed robbery in a coffee shop this morning."

"Good for you. Why aren't you at work yet?"

"I discharged my weapon. Twice."

There was a lengthy silence at the end of the line. "Anyone dead?" he finally asked.

"No, sir. Just two wounded."

"Even so. Lots of paperwork."

"I know, sir."

The shoot was justified, but Jessica knew her day was about to be busy with lots and lots of endless forms to fill out and reports to file, and her boss knew it, too. She lifted her eyes and stared across the room where Jones talked to a police officer.

A salacious memory of round three flew into her mind. She was straddled over Jones, his huge cock buried deeply inside her. She ground herself down and forward, then up, then down and backwards and up again. Then she continued the motion slowly, methodically, until his thumb suddenly brushed across her hot spot as she slid repeatedly over his flesh until—

Martin had just said something. She didn't know what, because she'd been daydreaming. No, she'd been remembering luscious things that should wait for later.

"What was that again, sir? It's a bit chaotic here."

"When will you be released from the scene? I need you here. I just got notified we're setting up for a joint task force. The principles in the case are out of Chicago, and due to arrive en masse early tomorrow. We need to be ready for them."

"I'll leave as soon as my replacement weapon is delivered. I understand it's on the way."

"You give your primary statement already?"

"Yes. The local PD can find me later if they need something else."

"Great." Martin hung up without further comment. He never said goodbye when he spoke on the phone, not even to his wife. Phone manners notwithstanding, he was a great boss.

His only fault, in her opinion, was that he was acquainted with her eldest brother, Jackson. The dream to escape her well-meaning brothers was thwarted even moving several states away. It also meant Martin treated her differently than all the other agents who answered to him. This earned her the title of Agent-in-Charge's Special Pet, courtesy of Neil Wiley.

Crap! She forgot. She had to face smarmy boy this morning, too. Her gaze crept back to Jones. He had one hand in his front pocket and the other held a cup of coffee. She had to hide the shudder of sexual desire that ran through her. It warred with her desire to get a sip of his coffee.

Jessica wanted Jones again. She wanted him tonight. The longer she stared at him, the more her desire rose. What if she took him to the coffee shop bathroom and had her wicked way with him and drank half his coffee before heading to work? That would definitely make it easier to face Neil.

"Isn't he gorgeous?" Kelli said in her ear.

"Yes. He is. But I already got laid."

"What?! When?"

"Saturday night after I left you at Joe's Bar. I'd planned on telling you this morning, but there was this little robbery."

"Oh. Then you don't need…" She gave a remorseful smile, "I'm so sorry, Jess. My mouth ran over as usual. I'll tell him—"

"No. Don't tell him anything. I appreciate you trying

to help, but I already told him the deed was done, and he was off the hook."

"Okay. So tell me, was this mysterious stranger any good?"

Jessica focused on Jones again. He looked up and gave her a devastatingly seductive smile before he saluted her with his coffee cup.

"He was amazing." She looked at Kelli, since she couldn't concentrate on anything but Jones's mouth. "Now I can face smarmy boy Neil today and get him out of my face, too."

"Will he believe you?"

"Actually, I don't care. I've put up with his shit long enough. If he gives me grief, I'll go to HR. He can't hide behind his nepotism forever, can he?"

"I hope not. You should have gone to them a long time ago."

"I know. I was afraid he'd win any HR battles. I thought I could ignore him. But he's gotten out of hand of late."

Kelli shrugged. "I only met him Saturday night and I want to kick his balls into his throat."

"Yeah? Get in line." She surveyed the scene before her. "That's probably why I should be a facial recognition analyst buried behind a desk doing reports and not a field agent. Also because I should have called for backup before charging in." They watched as the first wounded robber was carried out to a waiting ambulance.

"Don't be ridiculous. Thanks for saving me, Jessica. I truly thought he was going to kill me." Kelli was not a fragile flower, but the fear on her face when that thug had held a gun to her head made Jessica act instead of call for official help. She was lucky no one was dead, including her.

That reminded her. Someone had shoved her out of the way when the second gunman shot at her. She'd thought she was about to die. Who had saved her? Her eyes strayed to Jones. No. Surely not. But maybe. She scanned the area again, consulting her memory of the patrons' positions when she'd first entered. More than maybe, it was probable. Too bad she wasn't going to see him again or she'd ask.

"Agent Hayes," a new voice called out. She saw a man in an FBI jacket near the door and went to him. She signed several pieces of paper to take possession of the replacement piece. He gave her the gun butt first, and she secured in her shoulder holster.

She was back in business.

Kelli joined her as she adjusted her jacket to hide the bulge. "Are you going to be okay?" she asked her friend. "Do you want one of the paramedics to take a look at you?"

"No. I'm fine."

"Okay. Good. I hate to leave you, but I need to get to going. We should do this again, Kelli. But next time let's forgo the robbery, hostages and gunfire."

Kelli smiled. "I'm late for work, too. Meet me tomorrow morning right here and you can spill about your first time. Don't think you're going to get away without sharing some details." Kelli winked and walked away.

Not a chance. Jessica turned to take her leave of the officer in charge and walked straight into Jones's chest. Her hands went to his biceps to keep her balance and his arms came around her back under the guise of keeping her upright.

"God, you smell great," he whispered reverently. "Good enough to eat. Meet me tonight." His breath tickled her hair.

"No." But she couldn't seem to let go of him. Her fingers squeezed the muscles of his arms tighter. "Stop tempting me. I have to go to work. I'm late."

"Meet me tonight, Smith. Midnight. My place. I'll wait for you."

"I won't be there."

"I'll still wait. It's my night off."

"Let me go." She heard the desperation in her voice.

He pushed out a defeated-sounding sigh, and his arms dropped. Jessica held on to him a moment longer. The memory of all the sexual delights she experienced with him Saturday night pulsed through her. She swallowed hard and took a breath. With it came his scent. Her forehead leaned in to rest on his upper chest. *Oh my good heavens*, she wanted him so much.

"Okay. One more time." She tilted her head to look into his face, expecting to see a smug expression, but he looked relieved.

She reiterated, "But that's it. Just one more time."

A sexy half smile shaped his lips. "Until tonight then." He took a step back and she managed to release him. She cleared her throat and walked away without another word.

Jessica had a midnight date for hot fantasy sex.

Tonight could not come soon enough.

CHAPTER 4

Jessica entered the Federal Building hoping she wouldn't see Neil Wiley first thing, but it was Monday. Probably nothing was going to go the way she wanted it to today.

At least not until midnight.

She stepped off the elevator on the second floor to a sleazy-toned greeting. "Why, if it isn't little Miss Cherry."

"My name is Special Agent Hayes." She strode past Neil, refusing to look at him on her trajectory to her desk. He followed behind her. *Damn it.*

"I guess you won't be getting in trouble for being more than an hour late, since you're Special Agent-in-Charge Martin's special favorite pet, and oh so innocent, too."

Jessica turned to face him. "Whether I'm late or not is none of your goddamned business. And neither is my being *innocent*. I will repeat this only one more time. Do not ever approach me in a non-professional manner. Are we clear on this subject?"

He winked. "I know your little secret, Special Agent Hayes. I wanted to let you know that my offer is still open. Want me to stop by your place tonight and help you gain some experience? I'm sure I could open you up to a whole new way of life."

"No thanks. I already have plans."

"You don't need to lie to me, baby. I know you don't really have anyone to help you out. I fully understand that a woman like you has needs. I can help you. I promise it will be so good between us, baby." Neil leaned forward and put his slimy hand on her shoulder.

"I'll say it again. You are a co-worker. Do not ever approach me in a non-professional manner. I am not interested in you." She shrugged her shoulder to dislodge his hand. "Look at my face, Neil. I'm not lying. Get away from me. Stay away from me. And stop calling me baby, or so help me, I will make you regret it."

"Come on now. I can be reasonable. I'm only trying to help you." He placed his hand on her shoulder yet again. Jessica looked down at his sweaty, hairy hand. This time she removed it with her hand instead of shrugging it off. She also twisted it into a painful position until his knees buckled and he cried out.

Jessica released him and backed up a step. "Agent Wiley, this is my final warning. Get away from me. Stay away from me. Keep your hands off of me."

"Touchy, touchy," he said in a tone that suggested he thought he was very sexy. In a mock whisper, he said, "You desperately need to relax, Miss Cherry. Then you won't be so cranky and uptight."

Martin interrupted. "Agent Wiley, do you have this week's supply order complete?" Jessica had seen him approach, but hoped he hadn't heard Neil's last remark.

"Oh, uh, no," Neil stammered.

"Go do it now."

"Sure." Neil trotted off to his desk a couple of rows away. Thank heavens. Jessica was about to whip out her gun and shoot him, which would only add more paperwork to her life.

Martin crossed his arms and casually parked his hip on the edge of her desk. "Any fallout from the local police this morning?"

"Not yet. Why? Did you hear something?"

"No. But I will. I'll need your written account on my desk by end of day."

"You'll have it."

He nodded and gave her a concerned look. "You okay?"

"Yes, sir. I'm fine. Truly." She sought his eyes with hers when she added, "I'd also appreciate you not telling Jackson about this morning's incident if you happen to speak with him in the near future." All she needed was a worried call from her eldest brother to truly put her day in the toilet. If he was in a particularly ornery mood, she'd also get a call from her parents before the end of the day.

Martin smiled. They'd had this conversation before. He seemed compelled to share every minor paper cut she got at this job with her eldest brother. Then she'd get a long-distance call from him.

Jackson was an FBI assistant director in another state. She'd moved away to have her own life. She didn't want to have four overbearing brothers looking out for her. Jackson was the worst, especially since they were both in the Bureau.

"He worries about you."

"I know. But I'm old enough to take care of myself. While I understand you two are thick as thieves, sir, please don't rat me out about today's shooting."

He nodded. "You're right, it's not my place. I won't say anything. However, you should probably tell him yourself. If this story hits the national news—and it will—he'll find out for himself. Better he hears it from you first." She nodded, but didn't plan on telling Jackson anything. Martin gave her one last concerned look and then said, "Do you want to be on the task force?"

"More than anything in the world."

"Well, they want an on-site facial recognition analyst on the team. You may have to do some field analysis in the van."

"No problem. You know I won't sleep until the team leader has everything he needs."

"Good. You'll be working with Agent John Pierce. He's a hard-ass, but a good agent. You'll learn a lot from him."

"Great."

"Don't forget that incident report by end of day."

"I won't. Thanks for recommending me for the task force."

He nodded and sauntered back to his office. Jessica wanted on the task force more than she wanted coffee at this moment. And she wanted some caffeine in the worst way.

Once she was on the task force, the special agent-in-charge from Chicago would be her new boss until the task force concluded. Good or bad, she would be treated like an FBI agent instead of the baby sister of an old friend from school. She was sick to death of being overprotected by her brothers and having miniscule control over her life.

"Guess you and I will be working together." Neil was back. "I'm going to be on the task force too."

Jessica ignored him and started her computer. Damn it all to hell. How did he get to be on the task force? He must have called his uncle, the person responsible for Neil even having a job. He was the biggest screw-up the department had ever seen, at least in her jaded eyes. Neil abused his familial connection on a regular basis. Of course he was picked for the task force; his uncle made sure he got every premium assignment available.

Jackson tried to pull strings for her the first week, but she refused to let nepotism rule her life. Neil, on the other hand, wallowed in it. He didn't earn a single blessed thing by doing anything relevant. In her opinion, he was lucky he had a job at all.

"Maybe we'll get to spend some cozy time together on some overnight stakeouts."

Don't hold your breath, she thought angrily, refusing to look at him, talk to him or respond in any way. After several minutes, he finally got the hint and walked away.

Later in the cafeteria, Neil made a big stink about her shooting someone and made lots of references to *that time of the month* to what few friends he had left. She grabbed a sandwich to go and ate at her desk.

Other than Neil being a pain in her ass, Jessica's day went smoothly. It was late when she was ready to leave. She hadn't seen Neil in a while and hoped he'd gone home early, as usual.

She checked the time. Only five and a half more hours until midnight. Only five and a half more hours until she could have wild, wicked sex with her hot date.

Jessica thought about Jones periodically throughout the day—if periodically could be defined as every other minute. What was it about him that made her salivate and daydream?

She didn't even know who he was besides his name. Mark Reece. She didn't want to do a search in FBI files and learn he was a wanted man, a career criminal or, worse, married and lying about it. She checked all of the most wanted posters displayed in the cafeteria as she waited to pay for her sandwich. He wasn't on any of them.

Kelli knew him, so he likely wasn't a homicidal maniac or married. Her friend was mouthy, but had a strict moral code regarding wedding vows. Perhaps she'd ask Kelli for a few more details tomorrow morning. No, she wouldn't. She wasn't going to see him after tonight, so it didn't matter.

She just wanted to have sex one more time. She liked sex. She loved sex with Jones, but it didn't mean anything at all. They were going to scratch each other's itches one last time, perhaps even repeatedly, but only for one more night. She wondered what would happen if she showed up well before midnight.

Her craving would be fulfilled earlier, that's what would happen. Jessica glanced at her watch, scheming and planning the rest of her evening to meet earlier.

Reece glanced around his apartment to make sure everything was in place. Champagne. Chilled flutes. Appetizers. Flowers. He noted the time on the clock as he checked the atmosphere. Another minute had passed since he glanced the last time.

God, he was such a letch. No. He was anxious. He liked her. A lot. Too much, if she really didn't want to continue this affair.

He didn't know if his lovely gun-wielding FBI agent and recently deflowered virgin would even show up. He glanced at his watch yet again. Thirty-eight minutes until midnight. But he was ready. His cock began to swell at the mere thought of sex tonight after such a long dry spell interrupted only by last Saturday night's incredible sexcapades with the lovely Miss Smith.

He remembered again the sublime feeling of sinking into her wet, slick warmth. It had been indescribable. The prickly anticipatory sensation of, *I'm finally about to get my rocks off after months of zero action* had surrounded his dick as each subsequent inch penetrated her slowly and exquisitely, filling her to the hilt. It had been her very first time, which on some level made the memory even better. He'd never been anyone's first time before.

He didn't remember any stubborn resistance or any sort of hymen-tearing feeling, just that she was amazingly tight. Not that he had deflowered any virgins to know the difference. She hadn't cried out in agony as if he'd ripped her asunder with that first thrust.

She'd made sexy moaning noises. His cock throbbed, tightening his pants below the zipper, so he thought of something else. He reflected over this morning's adventures at the coffee shop.

Reece's mind had been on his lovely mystery woman as Kelli had described her very best friend Jessica, who needed to get laid for the first time. But Reece didn't want to have sex with anyone else.

He'd inhaled a deep breath to break the bad news to Kelli, *Sorry, no can do, I've got another woman on my mind,* when he'd heard an angry voice by the door say, "Get up. Hands in the air. This is a robbery. No one tries to be a hero and no one gets hurt."

Reece stood slowly along with his friends and the rest of the coffee shop clientele as two armed ski mask-wearing men proceeded to rob the place. He watched, wondering what he could do, or if he should do anything at all. No. He didn't want anyone to get hurt, but he couldn't break his deep undercover assignment even for an armed robbery. He didn't have his gun on him anyway.

The gunman closest to the front door abruptly turned his focus on Kelli. He approached her and made an overture.

"Hey, sexy girl. Want to go with us and spend our ill-gotten gains?" He then made disgusting kissing noises.

"Fuck off, pervert," Mike, his friend, had snarled in defense of Kelli. Then all hell broke loose. The gunman grabbed Kelli by the hair and pulled her close.

"I guess this means you'll be coming with us after all, sweetheart!" He wrapped an arm around her neck as Mike had gone rigidly angry and taken a step in their direction.

Reece shot him a look to calm him down as the gunman pointed his gun at Kelli's head, backing her away from the group.

"Anyone makes a move and I blow her head off!"

Reece readied himself to play concerned citizen. If Kelli was led out, he planned to follow at a discreet distance under the pretense of foolish citizen goes to help friend. But then a gorgeous FBI agent had foiled all the plans in motion, including his.

Smith saved his ass and ultimately his well-guarded cover by shouting, "FBI! Drop your weapon!"

Reece recognized her voice immediately.

The gunman holding Kelli had swung to face Reece's still unseen lover. Mr. Pervert Bad Guy raised his gun to shoot towards the front door. Reece tensed, because he couldn't see through the wall of planters with the damn six-foot high foliage in his way.

Bang!

He'd jumped at the sound of the gunshot and moved a step in the direction of the door, hands still in the air. He almost sighed with relief when the idiot slid to the floor with a leg wound gushing blood, screaming like a sissy about his injury. His girl had wounded one of the bad guys. His eyes widened even as his pride surged when the gunman poised at the register ducked behind the waist-high counter.

Smith. His gorgeous, wonderful Smith quickly moved into his visual range. Her hair was pulled back into a simple ponytail, and she was dressed in the sexiest figure-hugging black business suit he'd ever seen. She promptly kicked the first gunman's weapon out of reach. His eyes wandered down to the ass displayed perfectly below the hem of her jacket. Her luscious butt, the one he'd been in love with at first sight. His gaze scanned her body, the one she'd so generously shared with him repeatedly less than two days ago, called to him.

He subdued his desire to touch her when she backed up close enough to be within his reach. She glanced in his direction over one slim shoulder, her eyes scanning the crowd, and obviously saw no threat. Why would she? The threat was hiding. She couldn't see the other gunman. Didn't know he was there.

Reece sent her a mental warning, but too late. Everything happened in slow motion. He saw Smith drop her shoulders, relaxing her stance slightly just as the gunman by the register stood. His gun was leveled and ready to shoot. Reece reacted without thinking, shoving her shoulder, hoping he could save her.

Bang! The gunman fired, but because of his shove, the bullet meant for her heart missed her chest altogether. A bullet shouldn't ever mar that premium flesh.

Even as he connected, he knew he shouldn't have done it. He should have continued to be an alarmed coffee shop patron. But he was an undercover DEA agent and some things were too engrained to suppress, like saving a fellow law enforcement officer's life. Especially one he knew very intimately.

He was currently on a no-end-in-sight—already a year—undercover assignment as a bouncer for an upscale nightclub. He was supposed to only report on the club's activities to his higher ups. But if criminal scum came in and made deals in the club, he anonymously passed along their location to any agency searching for them.

In his current role as head breaking bad-assed bouncer, he shouldn't have the ready knowledge to determine probable shot and angle trajectory to remove her from the danger with a strategically aimed shove. So hopefully no one noticed his action. *Including his girl Smith.*

He had done a stint in the Army. He could trot that training out as an explanation if he had to, but didn't want to, as his current alias didn't have the documentation to support it.

After his little push, Smith went down on one knee, brought her service weapon up and shot the gun out of the hand of the man who'd tried to kill her. It was a damned fucking amazing shot. His respect for her escalated instantaneously and so had his lust. He wanted her. He was about to find out her true identity. Mentally, he rubbed his hands together in glee.

Smith, with her tasty flesh and uninhibited sexual appetite, had occupied his mind since he'd woken to find her gone Sunday morning. She hadn't left a note. No physical clue remained that she'd even been in his apartment, besides her delectable scent clinging to his sheets and the spicy taste of her lingering on his lips. And, of course, the telltale stains on his sheets. He tried to remember how many times they'd had sex. Was it four times or five? He had been afraid he'd been too rough with her. Afraid he'd fucked her raw.

Either way he *was* a barbarian, scowling when he woke up because he'd hoped to glean some pivotal information about her identity in between rounds of gratification, but failed.

After the first orgasm, he knew he wasn't ready to end the relationship. He'd expected her to run after the first amazing time while he was taking care of business in the bathroom. Even if she wanted only this one night, he most assuredly wanted more.

He'd memorized her license plate number when he changed the tire on her car. But his contacts at the Drug Enforcement Agency weren't easy to contact since he was, after all, undercover. To use his contacts, he'd have to invent a connection to the club. He didn't want his mystery girl on any watch list for the DEA. Besides, he wasn't supposed to be involved seriously with any women anyway. At least not unless it was a way to help do his job and further his UC assignment parameters.

Smith only furthered his personal boundaries. Exquisitely.

Soon after the police arrived at the coffee shop, he almost fell on the floor in shock as Kelli approached the wet-dream fantasy woman he knew only as Smith and called her Jessica.

Smith was Kelli's virgin friend? His mind went straight to the stained bed sheets he'd changed yesterday afternoon. He thought he'd been too aggressive. He thought he'd fucked his mystery girl so many times she'd bled from being overused. But no. She was a virgin. Well, not since he'd gotten hold of her...repeatedly. Less than forty-eight hours ago.

Now she was the only woman he could think of. She was the only woman in his personal history who brought his cock to immediate attention with only the mere thought of her. Memories of her face and body were what he'd jacked off to in the shower this very morning because he'd woken with a record-breaking hard-on.

When he glanced at her perfect ass after she'd shot the first bad guy, again his cock had stirred, ready for action. It was because before her, it had been such a long time. Surely his cock was merely showing supreme gratitude for ending the drought.

The first woman after so long without sex was always exceptionally satisfying, right? Or was it more than that? Was it a deeply important connection that he needed in his endlessly long, lonely undercover cop life feeling as forgotten as the last kid picked up after school?

Buzz. The intercom for the front door of his apartment building broke into his unwelcome musings. He checked the time as he crossed the room and punched the intercom button. She was twenty-six minutes early. That was a good sign.

"Yes!" His voice was too loud for a simple intercom connection. Did he sound desperate? Probably.

"It's me...Smith. I'm a little early." Her sweet voice sounded very tentative.

"No problem. Come on up. Eighth-floor, number eight thirteen. In case you weren't paying attention the last time."

Reece pressed the door release button. His heart pounded in his chest. He reminded himself that his plans tonight didn't include pouncing on her the moment she stepped inside his domain. He'd give her the flowers, they'd sip champagne, enjoy some appetizers, and then...then he'd pounce on her, if she was willing.

Ding-dong.

Reece strode to the door and wrenched it open on her surprised face. *Calm down.* He smiled and motioned her inside, holding the door open wide.

"Hi, Jones."

"Smith. Glad you could make it."

"I'm early. I hope that's okay."

"Early is great." She stepped up to him as he closed the door and wrapped her arms around his neck. The door snapped shut. He grabbed her close to his chest and planted his lips on hers. He devoured her as he'd been longing to do since the last time his mouth had been in the proximity of her lips.

Reece leaned back against the closed door, taking her with him. His hand strayed down to her ass and he rubbed one cheek, massaging it as he ground his pelvis into her. His cock was naturally already swollen, stiff and taking complete advantage of her open legs.

He raised his lips to tell her about the champagne, the flowers. "Smith?"

"What?" She trailed kisses across his jaw and he couldn't think. Her teeth nibbled a path along his jawline. She tugged his earlobe between her teeth in a nip that made him break out in a sweat.

"You taste good, and you feel even better." He tightened his grasp on her and lifted his hips into her again. She moaned and pushed back, making his cock swell even further. Was he about to burst? He took a breath to calm himself, but she spoke in an urgent, sexually charged tone.

"Oh, my good heavens, take me to bed, Jones. I'm going to die if you don't take me this instant."

Her mouth slid back to his and opened on his mouth. She brushed her tongue past his teeth to stroke against his deliciously.

"Well, we can't have that." He clutched her closer, lifted her legs off the floor and proceeded to carry her to his bed.

Eagerness pervaded all his senses, and he swore he saw red. Sexual red. He needed to get inside her. Now. He smiled and went through the doorway to his bedroom still kissing her luscious lips. His girl wanted the carnal activities to start first.

Everything else would have to wait.

CHAPTER 5

Jessica discovered an animalistic side she never knew she harbored. On the way up the elevator, she'd fanaticized about opening her legs and landing on Jones as soon as she was invited inside. The scrumptious scent of him hit her like a wall of sexual enticement. She launched herself at him the minute she crossed his threshold. This second she was naked, staring up at him from his bed, watching him strip as she licked her lips. As far as she was concerned, he couldn't get his dick inside of her fast enough.

"You look good enough to eat, Jones." She watched him falter a moment as a sardonic smile spread across his talented lips.

She thought of a certain sexual act she hadn't tried yet. Actually, she'd thought about it all day. She wanted to see what would happen if she sucked on his oh-so-very-impressive cock. Before she lost her nerve, she sat up, flung her legs over the edge of the bed and grabbed his hips to pull him toward to her face.

Jones made an inarticulate noise as she put her mouth on his stiff cock through his boxers. There was already a wet spot before her tongue hit him. She blindly felt for the elastic of his underwear and slipped her fingertips in the band to pull them down. His warm, smooth cock sprung free and skimmed her lips as if kissing her in pre-gratitude for what she was about to do.

Jessica hadn't a clue what she was doing. Acting on instinct alone, she placed her lips around his sizeable head and sucked him inside her mouth. She then licked the bottom part of his cock, pulling him as far into her mouth as he would go.

She placed a hand around the base of his shaft as his curly short hair tickled her pinky. The other hand rested on his hip. She squeezed the base of his shaft and along with the hand on his ass, used it as leverage to pull his cock back out of her mouth, keeping the suction tight. Jones growled and his legs trembled against her thighs where they were tucked intimately.

In response, she sucked him back in her mouth until the wide tip of him closed off her air. His hands were on her head suddenly, pulling her off.

She stopped and looked up past his muscular chest all the way to his face, which was a seriously lust-filled mask of unspent passion. He sank to his knees beside the bed. His mouth was on hers in a flash.

He pulled away and cupped her face in his hands. "That was," he sighed and rolled his eyes, "fucking amazing. But I don't want to come that way for this first time tonight. I need to sink deeply inside of you. Any problem with that?" He didn't take his eyes off her, but he reached unerringly for his bedside drawer, which she knew held his impressive condom stash.

"Nope. I'm all for it, Jones." She scooted backwards on the bed. He stood and she watched as he rolled the latex over his substantial erection. He immediately climbed on all fours over her.

"Let's try something new. Turn over, Smith."

Her eyes widened, but she rolled to her belly without comment. He came close behind her and lifted her to her knees so she pressed her shoulder blades against his chest. His hands went to her breasts and kneaded them softly. He ran his fingertips across her aching nipples, which distended to tingling buds as he played with her. His cock slipped between her legs. The heat of his hard flesh rested against the slit of her aching body. Her neck lost its ability to hold her head up and she leaned it back against him.

"You have the most beautiful body," he whispered.

His hands stroked the entire front of her. He massaged her breasts, then her belly, and then her hips. This before one hand went to the aching, needy place between her legs. She felt fingertips rub and play with her mound, swirling her hair around, but not touching her. Her hips pressed into his hand, trying to make the connection. He dodged her and rubbed her belly.

"Please. Please touch me." He kissed her face and tugged her earlobe with his teeth, sucking it between his lips as he slipped a finger down to her swollen clit.

"Oh my good heavens."

He slid his finger across her as one hand pinched and played with a nipple. Then he kissed the back of her neck in a newly discovered sensitive place, making her moan louder. His hips moved back and forth and his cock slid across her slick opening. His finger stroked her with increasing speed. He took a nip at the cord on her neck and the orgasm he brought on overwhelmed her almost without warning. She screamed in pleasure.

He pushed her facedown on the bed, tilted her hips up and entered her sweetly pulsating body to the hilt from behind. She moaned in delight as he pumped inside her with purpose, clutching her hips for leverage. She lost track of time as he moved within her body.

After enjoying every single moment of this blissful connection, she climaxed yet again. He continued thrusting inside of her deeply from behind, the angle driving her over the edge of bliss. Jones growled and pumped one final surging thrust as he bent over her, groaning. The crisp chest hair brushing her back tickled. He remained bent over her, gasping, and soon he trembled. His weight crushed her to the bed. She gave a muffled laugh.

He soon rolled to his side, his arm around her waist keeping them intimately connected as he took her with him. She could feel his heartbeat against her back. He brushed fingertips along the side of her face and then lightly skimmed his hand up and down her perspiration-covered body.

He lifted his head to kiss her cheek and hug her close before he slumped back to the bed.

"Thanks, Jones."

"My pleasure." His low voice rumbled in her ear. "You're amazing." He kissed her again, took a deep breath and slid out of her. He slowly made his way to the bathroom, winking at her once over his shoulder.

Jessica rolled off the bed, suddenly feeling energized. She snagged his shirt off the floor and put it on, rolling the sleeves up. She felt like the ultimate sex kitten dressed in his shirt. He came out of the bathroom and smiled at her attire.

"That's my shirt you're wearing, Smith. Not surprising that it looks better on you." He approached her in all his glorious nakedness. She glanced between his legs, surprised to see him soft for the first time since they'd met.

"Thanks. Makes me feel sexy."

"You are definitely sexy, with or without that very lucky shirt covering you. By the way, I have something for you in the dining room."

He scooped his pants and boxers off the floor and donned them quickly. He then led her to his dining room. There was a large spray of what had to be at least two-dozen mixed color roses in a vase. There was a bucket with a bottle of champagne, iced and ready.

He disappeared into what she presumed was the kitchen when he reappeared with two chilled champagne flutes. He grabbed the bottle, removed the foil, popped the cork and poured them each a glass.

"To excellent scratching." She held up her glass in salute.

"And hopefully to more of it." He clinked his glass against hers.

She took a sip. It was sweet, crisp and very good.

"Are you hungry?"

"Famished." Jessica couldn't remember her last meal.

He took her hand and led her into his kitchen. From the refrigerator he pulled out a platter with a variety of cheeses, sliced meat and fruit decoratively placed alongside sliced bread and crackers.

"Thanks." She made a little sandwich and studied him as he leaned against the small kitchen island where he'd placed the food and munched on crackers.

"Did you ever get through all that paperwork?"

"No. Just the initial incident report. Likely it'll seem like a forever project, with a minimum of two to three weeks before the conclusion. But on a brighter side, I'm starting an exciting new project soon."

"Awesome. Wait—am *I* the exciting new project?" He gave her a devastatingly sexy smile.

She took a long sip of champagne and murmured, "No, but you're running a close second."

"I'd like to keep seeing you Smith, but I don't want to scare you off or press you into something you don't want."

She studied him. He was fabulous, perfect even. She'd be stupid to relinquish him so soon. She should find out more about him before making any snap judgments about him based on the amazing sex they had together.

"Saturday night you told me you had women throwing themselves at you at work. Will you tell me what your job is?"

"I guess that's fair since I know yours now. I'm a bouncer at the Lexicon Club."

"A bouncer?"

"Well, technically my title is security specialist, but I was never one to put on airs."

She gave him a once over. He looked exactly like a bouncer. A gorgeous one. She'd be willing to bet women offered all manner of enticements to get into the most exclusive club in the city.

"Disappointed in my career choices, Smith?" He ate another cracker and took a sip of his drink. But he watched her closely, as if steeling himself for a negative response.

"No, not at all. I was just thinking about all those women who offer to do exactly what I did tonight so they can get to the head of the line and into your club faster." She lifted her eyebrows in question.

"I told you, I always turn them down."

"Hmm. Really? Always? You've never taken anyone up on it?"

She saw a flash of something in his eyes. Regret? Sorrow? Pain? But just as quickly as it appeared, it was replaced by a mischievous expression.

"Okay, in the name of full disclosure, I did make one mistake a very long time ago that I've sworn I won't repeat. There was a woman. She fooled me, which isn't easy to do. She wanted easy access to the club. I was her way inside. Turns out we weren't exclusive like I thought. In fact, she had the hots for just about every other guy available within her airspace." He shrugged, but she could tell it had hurt him to some degree.

"I see. So I shouldn't expect to gain access to your club." Again that flash of sorrow, as if he thought of something completely distasteful then thrust it from his mind. She certainly understood what kind of effect that could have on a person.

He grinned. "Of course I'd let you in, Smith. Do you like to dance?"

"No. I'm not a party, dance-club sort of girl." She shrugged. She'd always hated the club scene. "Remember when I promised you the first night we were together that I wasn't looking for a boyfriend?"

"Yes."

"I'm reconsidering my options."

"Are you? Excellent. I believe that it's always a woman's prerogative to change her mind. I'm open to furthering our acquaintance, Smith, if that's what you're suggesting."

"Well, I'm still not looking for a steady boyfriend, but I must admit that I would like to see you again, too."

"Then why don't you come with me to my club tomorrow night? I'm off duty again like tonight, but one of the perks I rarely take advantage of is getting in on my nights off."

"Your club?" She shrugged again. "Okay. However, now I'm obligated to give you full disclosure, too. I'll warn you up front, I don't dance."

He glanced down her body and back up again with leisurely intent. "Well, the kind of dancing I want to do with you doesn't take much skill. We'll just press our bodies together and sway back and forth to the soft beat of the music. Tell you what, I'll lead."

"Deal." Jessica looked down at her watch and couldn't believe how late it was.

They pulled out their cell phones and exchanged numbers. She promptly tapped in "Jones" next to his. He showed her that he'd labeled her number "Smith" in his contacts. It pleased her. It was something they shared together.

"I need to go. I have a big day tomorrow, which starts with Kelli at the coffee shop."

"I may see you there. Mike and I meet for coffee every morning. I don't want you to think I'm stalking you."

"But this," she pointed between them, "stays between us, yes?"

"Yes. Don't forget, though, the club is a public place."

"But our friends, especially Kelli, don't need to know how we met or what we already are to each other."

"True." His brows furrowed. "And what is that specifically?"

Her face warmed. "Already very intimate."

"Got it. We just met at the coffee shop robbery and now we're friends."

"With benefits."

"Fuckin' A."

"But we don't kiss and tell."

"Of course not. Why would we do that?"

Jessica moved into his personal space and kissed him like she didn't want to leave. She didn't. But ten minutes later, she reluctantly released him, strolled back to the bedroom to get dressed in her own clothes, and regretfully left his shirt behind on the bed.

"I'll keep it for you to wear the next time you're here," he said from the doorway. The bare skin of his gorgeous, well-sculpted chest tempted her to blow off Kelli in the morning and entice him to make love to her once more. As if he read her mind, he offered, "I could tell Mike I can't make it tomorrow if you'd like to stay a little longer tonight."

"I would, but I really do have a big day at work tomorrow, and that new special project. I don't want to be sleep deprived. And we both know I would be."

He nodded. "You're absolutely correct."

She'd better leave now. He snagged the shirt she'd left on his bed and slipped it on, sniffing the collar as if her scent lingered there. He escorted her across his apartment, holding her close as if she were precious. At his front door, he kissed her tenderly once before opening it.

When he followed her out into the hallway, she frowned.

"I know you can kick ass and everything, but I'd feel better if I walked you to your car, since it's so late."

Jessica didn't mind. They went hand in hand to the elevator, embraced in one corner all the way to the ground level and, true to his word, he walked her to her car.

"You need to get that tire changed to a real one."

"No doubt, but I'm busy."

"Just be careful. No car chases for you, right?"

She snorted. "See you later, Jones."

"Until tomorrow, Smith." He grabbed her hand and kissed it. She paused a second to smile at him before she stepped into her car, pulling her hand away so she didn't change her mind, follow him back inside and stay the night. She wanted to. Very much.

She watched in her rearview mirror as he walked back to his building. He looked up at the surrounding buildings as if searching to see if someone had watched them together. Interesting because she'd felt like someone had watched her early Sunday morning when she snuck out of his apartment.

Jessica shivered for no reason and departed the area quickly, heading home. Tomorrow would be challenging enough and now memories of Jones would slip in if she wasn't valiant in her efforts to be a consummate professional.

Jessica met Kelli the next morning at the scheduled time. She ordered her regular large mocha, which the clerk told her was on the house because she thwarted the robbery the day before. She turned and saw Jones with the same guy as yesterday. He pretended to talk to his friend, but she'd seen several glances come her way while she waited for her coffee.

She caught Kelli's wave from across the room and walked over to her table.

"So what do you think of Reece?" Kelli asked before Jessica even sat down.

"I thought his name was Mark."

"Oh. It is, but everyone calls him by his last name, Reece." Kelli frowned. "I think he used to be in the Army a long time ago or something. Maybe it's a military thing. I don't know."

Jessica had always called him Jones. Perhaps she'd call him Reece tonight and see if he noticed. She seated herself at the table so her view would include Jones. She wanted to watch him. Probably juvenile, but whatever.

Kelli was still talking. "...even though you already got rid of your virginity with someone else. Reece is a good choice to be the next man in your life." Jessica didn't disagree that Reece was an exceptional man. But she was unsure of how to tell Kelli—or if she even should—that she wasn't interested in making time for a relationship.

Perhaps she should back away slowly from the almost relationship with him now that the light of day gave her sudden rationality. But then Jones turned a very seductive gaze her way, giving her a bad boy half smile. The one that said, "I've seen you naked, I've made you scream in pleasure, and I can't wait to do it again."

She shook off his blatantly possessive stare and asked, "How do you know him?"

"He takes classes at the local community college where I'm taking that business course."

"He's a college student?" Jessica hadn't seen that coming.

"Yeah. If it weren't for him I would have failed my required Business Law class."

"Really?" Jessica glanced at him, trying to be cool. He still watched her intently. She took a longer look across the room, returning the heated lip-licking gaze he sent her way. A bouncer with an aptitude for Business Law. How extraordinary was that?

"You should talk to him, Jess. He got dumped by some chick over a year ago because she only wanted to use him to get into his club. There was apparently more to it, but he never talks about her. And that doomed relationship has kept him out of the game. She was vile, but he's such a great guy. Don't discount him because I screwed up."

"I'm sure he is great." *I know for a fact he's a premium male specimen in bed and likely out of it.* The girl who'd pretended they were exclusive, but didn't follow through was the bad memory she'd noticed flash across his face the night before. "I promise to give him a chance, but not now. Perhaps I'll talk to him later. I need to get to work."

"Reece is as gun-shy as you are regarding relationships. I know! Why don't I set something up?"

"Like what?" Jessica wasn't certain she wanted to engage with him publicly just yet. She'd have to hold back and not slither over to him on her hands and knees begging for it, like she already wanted to do this morning.

"Like a double date."

"A double date? Who are *you* going with?"

Kelli glanced over at the other table. "I want Mike in the worst way. He broke up with someone a while back, and I believe it's time he was with a new woman. I'd like to fulfill his rebound lover requirements."

"You're shameless."

Kelli lifted one shoulder unapologetically. "Maybe I just go after what I want."

Jessica couldn't help looking at Jones again. His eyes met hers, like he sensed them on him. He gave her another positively bone-melting grin when he caught her gaze. He looked at her in the way a man does when he has intimate knowledge of a woman. He did. Jessica wasn't immune. She also wanted him in the worst way…again.

"I want Mike to look at me the way Reece is staring at you right now. It looks like he can't wait to get you alone, but he'd probably never approach you unless pushed." Kelli let out a very vocal sigh. "Let me be the one to push them both."

Jessica nodded, but cautioned, "Okay, but don't set anything up just yet. I'm about to be engrossed at work on a special project for a minimum of a week."

"No promises. I need to grab Mike before someone else snaps him up."

Jessica rolled her eyes, but then gave Jones a particularly salacious grin on her way out, including a slow swipe of the tip of her tongue over her bottom lip and a saucy wink.

CHAPTER 6

When she got to work, Jessica wrapped up several other projects or found others to hand them off to so she'd be available to do whatever was needed for the task force leader, Agent John Pierce. The hard-ass she would learn a lot from, according to her boss. That was good. She liked learning things.

The task force from Chicago had gone directly to a field operation site away from the Federal Building to set up surveillance from the primary watch post. They were due to arrive later in the day to brief the local reinforcements for further tasking. Jessica lingered at her desk, dreading the fact that Neil was on the team, too.

He eventually found her alone late in the morning. "So, Miss Cherry, you look relaxed today."

Jessica didn't respond or look up. She wanted to say, "I'm relaxed, you idiot, because I found an incredible lover. And he *made love to* me last night to my repeated pleasure." But she didn't. She ignored the smug bastard, delighting in the fact that it seemed to annoy him more than she'd ever seen before.

He made several attempts to engage her, but she didn't rise to the bait, pretending he wasn't even there.

Eventually he got bored and left. Thank the heavens above for small favors.

She was working through lunch finishing up various small projects when a commotion drew her attention to the elevators.

The Chicago task force had arrived. They marched in unison two abreast, two rows down the hall toward the cubicle farm where she worked. They were all dressed in dark suits and light shirts. No-nonsense apparel. If they'd sported sunglasses and hats, she would have thought a Blues Brothers look-alike contest had just descended on their Federal Building.

One man broke into the lead, approaching her down the long row of desks. He had to be Pierce. He had very blond hair, ice-blue eyes she could see even from this distance, and an expression of *I'm-in-charge-here* arrogance she recognized from hard-ass men very much like her brother Jackson.

It was the perpetual scowl that gave him away. If he ever smiled it would be only in triumph over a defeated foe but the amusement would never reach his gaze, instead being chillier than any iceberg in the North Atlantic.

Martin met him halfway down the hall, shook hands with him and directed them all to the Arlington conference room. He signaled her to join the group. Jessica stood up and made her way to the room.

Unfortunately, so did Neil. Steps before the doorway, he came up behind her and brushed his hand across her ass.

"Hey!" Jessica turned, ready to clock him.

"Jeez, you really need to relax, Miss Cherry. It was an accident." Neil's mocking petulant face made her want to throttle him, but she marched into the Arlington room, fuming. *Calm down.*

She waited until Neil found a seat and then took the one furthest from him.

Her boss sat next to her. "Agent Pierce, I'd like to introduce you to the members of our staff who'll be helping you with this task force." He introduced Jessica, three others from various departments and the idiotic bane of her existence, Neil.

Pierce introduced Agent Rick Gordon, a tall, nice-looking Asian-American, as his right-hand guy and two others, a dark-haired woman named Elsa Davis and a very young blond computer tech named Seth Bell, mentioning in his introduction that he was a genius with any and all things computer related or digital.

Pierce started talking, and Seth had slides up on the big screen as he uttered his first words. "The central office was notified anonymously that a sleazy criminal our team has been after for quite some time was recently seen in a local club. This is where we've already set up initial surveillance. It's a very exclusive, upscale nightclub. A confidential informant on someone else's payroll has alluded to a meeting between our guy and the owner of the club, who's purported to be a money launderer."

Jessica looked at the screen. The slide was of a very nice building at night with subtle lights outlining the shape. It looked like they'd taken the picture from across the street.

The place looked exactly like a high-end nightclub. Actually, it looked familiar. She leaned forward, focusing intently on the image.

The next slide was put in place. Pierce said, "Here's a clearer shot. Actually, do we have video available, Seth?" Seth's fingers moved like lightning across his keyboard. A video popped up on the conference screen.

It was a close-up of the large entry door, lit up on either side with subdued neon colors alternating blue, red and purple and then repeating. A line of people along the left side of the block waited to gain entrance. The building itself took up an entire block and the door resided on the corner. Her focus zeroed in on the white lights spelling out the name in big letters over the entryway, jolting her back in her seat. Her spine went ramrod straight.

The Lexicon Club. *Shit.* That was the place where Jones was a bouncer.

The next slide showed two men from a distance standing guard in front of the club. Pierce sent an intense stare down the table. "Here are the club's two primary bouncers. Memorize these faces. They aren't wanted for any crimes at this point. They have never been arrested for anything. They are, however, at the very top of the security hierarchy there." Another slide flashed into place. It almost looked like a jail photo, but was likely a badge picture. "This is Hector Guzman." Another slide. Another badge picture. "And this is Mark Reece." The breath she inhaled in shock was likely heard on the other side of the building, but no one said a word.

Another slide flashed up on the screen. But this one was quite different.

Jessica stared at the image in abject horror. It was a grainy black and white photo—presumably zoomed in from a distance—of her and Jones exiting his apartment last night. They were holding hands, crossing the street, heading to her car. Another slide appeared. A shot of her car's license plate filled the screen before the next slide showed a close-up of Jones with his mouth pressed to the backs of her fingers right before she got into her car. His expression filled the entire screen with the look of a man who's just had intimate knowledge of a woman. If the angle had been right, they'd have caught her staring back with an equally satisfied look.

"What in the hell *is* this?" she asked out loud to no one in particular.

"Interesting reaction, because that's also my question," Pierce said. "What the hell are you doing in the company of *this* guy?" He nodded at Seth and another slide popped up on the large screen. It was of this morning at the coffee shop in the exact moment she gave him that saucy wink before exiting.

Jessica stared at Martin. He was obviously as surprised as she was. Her focus then went to Pierce. "That is none of your business." Her tone was harsh and angry from shock, and she didn't care.

"You're right, it's not. But I'm about to make it my business."

"What does that mean?"

"Obviously, you have a relationship with this man. You are not being asked to disclose the specifics. However, I'm hoping you'll help us get into the club in a much easier fashion than we'd initially planned."

Jessica opened her mouth, but words escaped her. They wanted her to use him? She shook her head, unable to speak just yet.

Pierce continued. "We *could* go the whole time-consuming—and very expensive, I might add—route of setting up an undercover operative to get inside and assess the place. You know, like where the vile bad guy we're trying to catch will be sitting to discuss all of his nefarious plans. However, since you have a more readily available way to gain entrance to this very exclusive club, we'd like to use your cachet if at all possible. So is it, Agent Hayes? Possible?"

She swallowed hard. What he asked wasn't completely unreasonable, but she was still reeling from being caught practically with her pants down in regard to her secret love affair. One she hadn't even truly committed to yet.

If she did fess up, her options of disclosure were limited. She refused to admit that he'd only started out as a one-night stand to remove her virginity or rather a two-night stand, because the first time had been so amazing. Or she could say they were a couple with a budding romance and agree to this crazy plan. But then she'd have to use a guy who'd been used before in this exact manner.

Neil managed to snort loudly from across the table. "You're with *that* guy? I don't believe it for a minute. You were a virgin looking to hook up for the first time only last weekend."

Jessica stood up, eyes on Neil, ready to burn her career to the ground. Because that's what would happen if she followed through on the tempting vision of launching herself down the conference table, using a military crawl on hands, belly and knees to reach Neil, wrap her fingers securely around his throat and strangle him in front of half a dozen federal agents.

In the next second, though, Pierce saved her the trouble.

"That is a wildly inappropriate remark, Agent Wiley," Pierce said coldly. He snapped his fingers loudly and pointed at Neil. "You are off the team. Get out of my meeting this instant!"

Neil, who'd been looking rather proud of himself for outing her most closely held secret, looked confused. "What?"

"What part of *get out of my meeting this instant* do you not understand? Go. You aren't needed here any longer."

"Do you know who I am?" Neil puffed up, looking like he did when anyone challenged him for being an ass.

Pierce stood. "I don't care who you are. Get out! Or else I'll make you get out."

Neil got to his feet, glared at Jessica like she was the one who caused his humiliating departure, and stalked from the room, slamming the door on the way out like a petulant child. In an instant, Pierce became her new favorite person in the world.

He turned to her immediately and said, "I'm sorry for his unfortunate and outrageous comments. I'm hoping you won't hold them against me. I'm not trying to get into your personal business, Agent Hayes. I'd just like to get inside that club and possibly plant some listening devices without anyone employed there knowing what we're doing. We could take a chance on trying to get in like anyone else does, but my understanding of this club is that it's *very* difficult to gain entrance. That is, unless someone already has an in. I believe that you possess that critical piece of our tactical strategy. Will you help us?"

Jessica took a deep breath and sat back down. She wanted to be a team player. She was grateful to Pierce for getting rid of Neil after only a single inappropriate remark. But what he was asking her to do was personal. She didn't know Mark Reece that well. She hated to use him at this point in their relationship, especially considering what she knew about his history.

"Are you asking me to try and get inside with another man on my arm? Because I'm fairly sure that might end our new relationship rather quickly."

"Of course not. You and your new best girlfriend Elsa will head inside there to dance the night away."

Jessica closed her eyes. "It won't work."

"Why not?"

"I already told him I'm not a club girl. He knows I hate loud club scenes and that I don't dance. He's invited me inside as his guest, but—"

"Really? When?"

She cleared her throat. "Well, tonight actually. I agreed to go in and get drinks, but—"

"Perfect."

"How is it perfect? I don't think he'd buy me scurrying off to plant bugs with my friend as reasonable behavior."

"Perhaps you could call him, tell him the date's off

unless you can bring your old college roommate Elsa and *her* date Gordon, who arrived in town at the last minute. Do you think he'd agree to bring them along to the club if the alternative is no date at all?"

"Would you?"

Pierce shrugged. "Maybe." He looked over his shoulder at the picture of Jones kissing the backs of her fingers. "In this particular photo, he looks very interested in you, if you don't mind me saying. I think he'd do anything for you if he could."

Jessica did not want to test her ability to keep Jones interested, but it was likely he'd agree since he was the one who wanted to keep seeing her when she balked. She pushed out a long breath. "Okay. I guess—"

"Excellent."

"Wait."

"We don't have much time, Agent. Can you call him?"

She blanched. "Right now?"

"Yes."

Jessica stuttered. "This relationship is…" *How can I put this without confirming Neil's very accurate accusation?* "Well, let's just say we haven't been seeing each other for very long." *Try less than a week.*

"I see that as a plus. He'll be trying harder to keep you interested."

She was about to ask how when the door to the conference room opened and Martin's executive assistant stepped inside, leaned down and whispered in her boss's ear.

His eyes widened. He turned to her. "Agent Hayes has a visitor."

"Who is it?" she asked.

Margaret said, "There's a Mr. Mark Reece downstairs in the lobby asking to speak to you."

CHAPTER 7

Reece wasn't usually so forward when it came to new relationships and women. He also shouldn't have his ass currently parked, waiting in the fucking Federal Building lobby, seeking the company of his latest love affair. But this visit onto her turf wasn't his call.

He wanted to talk to her, just not with ulterior motives guiding him as they did today. It had been made clear to him what he must say and do, whether he liked it or not, and he didn't.

Last night, after seeing her to her car, he'd gotten the weirdest feeling of being watched. He didn't see anyone, but that turned out not to mean a single damn thing. The phone call once he'd gotten back to his apartment this morning after coffee with Mike had changed everything.

He hated making the bold decision to just show up at her workplace, knowing Jessica was already very skittish about their relationship, but ultimately he had to guard his cover.

In fact, he'd already been verbally reprimanded for resisting this maneuver and promptly ordered to do it against his better judgement. There was no denying that Mark Reece needed to establish their relationship very clearly. It needed to be a very romantic relationship. It had to be a very *public* romantic relationship because it already *was* a fact in certain governmental agency circles.

Reece had been contacted by Miles Turner, his handler for this clandestine job, under the orders of several other members of his chain of command early this morning. He'd been linked to her at the coffee shop robbery through the paperwork and the media coverage much faster than he'd been prepared for.

The robbery had sent up a big red flag. Then another lettered agency—he didn't even know which one— snapped a picture of him and Jessica together last night and promptly entered that photo into a particular database where criminals were often hunted for or linked as associated in some way with other criminals.

He wasn't a criminal, but he did have a few unsavory ties within the parameters of the club as a part of his street cred. This indelibly linked him and Jessica together for the time being.

It had also led to this morning's emergency call from Miles, who wanted to know what the fuck he was doing with an FBI agent while undercover for the DEA.

No one *seemed* to know they'd spent Saturday night together, but he couldn't rule it out. Maybe they just hadn't played that card yet. For now, as far as everyone knew they'd met at a robbery on Monday morning. She was publicly established as FBI, but she did not know *his* true vocation. Then they'd met at his place that same night and been filmed leaving together very early the next morning when he walked Jessica to her car.

The powers that ruled over his career decided immediately that they wanted Reece to use Jessica for *his* undercover operation. He was to establish their relationship and then tell anyone in his fake undercover world who wanted the information that he had an "in" with a federal employee. The very idea of it made his skin crawl, but he wasn't in a position to argue. Reece was supposed to tell his club owner boss, Travis Arthur, that his girlfriend had access to any and all field operations information.

Therefore, she would be able to warn the club and its owner if any lettered agencies were going to be sneaking around. This was a very valuable connection for him, especially at this juncture of the seemingly endless undercover job.

Still, he hated to use her in this way or in any way. The only good news was perhaps they wouldn't have to sneak around to be together. That would be fine with him. He wasn't certain if it would be fine with her. And above all else he was *never* to tell her he was an undercover agent. *Ever.*

There were violent and actionable resources that would be used against him if she ever even suspected he was undercover law enforcement. Those resources were made very clear to him, repeatedly. It didn't matter if she was a fellow law enforcement officer. *Do not tell her* was supposed to be his new mantra. He'd added on the word "yet" to the end of his new mantra.

Across the vast lobby of the Federal Building, Reece saw Jessica exit from the area of the elevator banks. A horde of other people came behind her as she headed in his direction. She walked through security and made a beeline for him. Her expression was closed off, hard to read. She might be pretty angry with him for showing up this way. He didn't blame her.

The moment she was within speaking range, she said, "I didn't expect to see you here today." *Oh, yeah. She is pissed.*

"Honestly, I didn't expect to be here either. But something occurred to me and I felt I needed to be bold in this particular case."

She crossed her arms, blocking off any sort of hug or embrace. "What brings you here, Reece?" *Shit.* She'd used his real name. He briefly paused to enjoy the way she said it, though. It was the first time she'd called him anything but Jones.

"I wanted your car keys so I could take your vehicle to get the flat tire repaired. I know you're busy, but I'm off today. It would be no problem for me."

The expression on her face shifted from wary to utter disbelief. It was the only thing he could think of in an attempt to endear her affections. Plus, he truly did believe she was driving around unsafely on that temporary tire.

"What?" She shook her head. "Why would you do that?"

"Because I care about you. What if you need to be in a car chase later? You'd be up shit creek without a paddle."

Her lids narrowed, but he sensed she was softening. "How do you know the donut is still on my car?" Her eyebrows lifted, and he could definitely tell she was not as angry as when she'd first arrived.

"Isn't it?" She scowled, and he knew he was right. He'd gambled she wouldn't have had time to have it replaced on her way to work after leaving the coffee shop earlier.

He leaned closer. "I know for a fact that the donut is still on your car because I saw your vehicle at the coffee shop this morning. Before you tell me it could be another car, I memorized your license plate for fun. So please, let me take it and get it fixed. It's a safety thing."

"Really? That's the only reason you came in here today?"

He shrugged and rolled his eyes. "Okay. I also wanted to see if you were really an FBI agent."

Her brows furrowed once more, but her expression lightened considerably. "You didn't believe I was in the FBI? Why not? I flashed my badge at the coffee shop. Not to mention the local cops take a dim view of people who *claim* to be an FBI agent and start shooting up the place."

He shrugged. "Well, I didn't see your badge up close and personal. Could've been a fake. Trust me, I know all about fake IDs in my line of work. But since you didn't show it to me I couldn't be sure, now could I?"

A smile shaped her lips. *Fuck, she is stunning.* Jessica took a step closer, coming into his personal space. "So what I'm hearing is that the next time we're alone together you want me to show you my badge so you can get a good look at it?"

"Yes," he whispered, leaning forward to add, "and if you're wearing *only* my discarded shirt at the time, that would be awesome."

"Well, I'll have to think about it. Naturally, I don't show my badge to just anyone."

"What if I said please and then went and got your tire fixed for you?"

Jessica giggled. "You are something else." She looked over her shoulder, probably checking to see if anyone listened in. No one was within fifteen feet of them.

"I do my best."

"Fine. I'll show you my badge the next time we're alone...and I'm wearing your discarded shirt."

"Excellent. Now give me your car keys so I can be a hero and I'll be on my way."

She reached into her pocket and pulled out a key fob with a single key. Handing it to him, she held his fingers briefly before letting go.

"When do you get off work?" he asked quietly.

"Usually six, but I'm not certain about today."

"Oh, right, because you have that special project. The one you need extra sleep for. Is that right?"

She stared intently into his eyes for the first time since meeting him in the lobby. "Yes. That's exactly right."

"But we *are* still going out to my club tonight to dance, right? Please say yes."

That seemed to startle her. The powers ruling his life wanted them together in the club as soon as possible to establish him as linked to her in an intimate way. He was supposed to make a big show of having her on his arm, introducing her around to his fellow employees. He had no doubt that Jessica would loathe any special attention.

"Yes. But maybe we can just sit and have drinks."

Reece wasn't going to let her be a wallflower. Well, Reece Langston would have, but Mark Reece needed to establish her as a love interest. Being seen dirty dancing with her in the center of the club was his best option. "Oh no. We need to get on the dance floor at least once. I need one sexy slow dance around the room at the very least, maybe two. Don't make me look bad in front of my club friends."

She pushed out a sigh. "Okay. Just remember I don't dance, so you'll have to lead." Her head tilted back and she stared deeply into his eyes. She seemed distracted. Or was that regret he saw?

"I can't wait. I promise to make you look great on the dance floor."

She huffed. "That will be a tall order."

"Don't worry. I'm up for it."

"Of that I have no doubt." She gave him that same seductive look she had at the coffee shop this morning. The tip of her tongue touched the center of her top lip briefly and he wanted to press her to the marble floor of this busy Federal Building and have his wicked way with her.

"Watch it. I'm a mere mortal man and I love your sweet tongue."

She grinned, but stopped teasing him. "Sorry. I lost my head and forgot where I was. You make me want to do wild things. Guess I'll have to keep my eye on you."

"That's probably a good idea. So, shall I pick you up at your place tonight?"

Her gaze went to one side, as if she was about to make an excuse to call it all off. He held his breath, but soon she shrugged. "Sure."

Reece frowned. "You aren't afraid to give me your address, are you?"

Jessica shook her head in amusement. "No."

"Good. Because I'd planned to plunder your glovebox to find out where you live when I get your tire fixed anyway."

A mischievous smile surfaced. "Sorry. That won't help you. In fact, you'd end up at my parents' house several states away. But I'm sure my dad would *love* to talk to you."

"Ooh. That might be a little awkward."

She glanced around again as if doing a quick perimeter check to ensure their limited privacy. "Did I mention that I'm the youngest of five *and* the only girl?"

"Wow. You have four brothers, too?" he asked and then cursed himself. Reece Langston had four brothers. Mark Reece did not. He was about to change the subject and hope she didn't bring it up again but her focus was elsewhere. An arrogant-looking guy with a determined expression headed in their direction at a fast clip.

Jessica went a bit pale. From several yards away and closing fast, the man gave Reece a dirty look and shouted, "Agent Hayes, you're needed upstairs right now."

Jessica watched Neil's approach with active horror. He yelled out her name across the lobby, intruding on their quiet conversation, and advanced on the two of them with a particularly triumphant look in his eyes. What was he up to?

In as tolerant a tone as she could muster, she waved him off and said, "I'll be up in a few minutes." She still had to broach the subject of inviting her fake college roommate with a tagalong fake boyfriend out with them tonight. It was supposed to be their first night out together and not the perfect time to bring along anyone else in her opinion, but she'd be overruled again if she brought it up.

Neil scowled at Reece, stepped way too close to the two of them, and said, "No. Come right now."

He reached for her like the smarmy dirt bag he was. Reece suddenly moved in close, putting himself directly in her path. Neil's hand landed on Reece's jacket sleeve instead.

"Hands off of me, dude," Reece said over one shoulder. Neil snatched his hand back, watching Reece half cradle her in his arms with a most obvious and inappropriate jealous expression plastered on his face.

"Run along, little man. This is a private conversation. I'll think about sending her back upstairs when I'm through with her."

Neil's face went tomato red and his lips trembled in rage. "You...she...I..." He took a deep breath and tried again. "This is her place of work, she's needed upstairs, and there is an unwelcome guest here currently."

Jessica started to speak, but Reece's arm tightened around her shoulder. She closed her lips firmly to keep from screaming. Reece hugged her even closer to his warm side. "You are absolutely correct that there are one too many people standing here. And I hate to say this, but it's you, little man. So go away."

Jessica hugged closer to Reece, resting her head on his muscular shoulder. Neil turned and stomped off like the villainous cardboard character that he was, probably to plot more mayhem and give her grief. But at least he was off the team until he got his uncle involved. It probably wouldn't be long before she was dodging him again, but she'd enjoy the reprieve for as long as it lasted.

Lifting her head to stare deeply into Reece's eyes, Jessica realized this was not the time to bring up the change of plans for their evening. She'd wait and spring it on him when he came to pick her up. She operated on only a gut feeling, but went with it for the moment.

Instead of going back to the conversation about tonight's date, she asked, "How long will you have my car?"

"Not too long. Two hours tops."

"Okay." She squeezed his arm. "And thank you."

"Like I said, it's a safety thing."

"No. I meant, thank you for keeping Neil from touching me."

Reece's expression hardened. "Has he been bothering you?"

"Yes. He has." *But you give me strength.*

"I can make sure he never does it again."

"So can I." She lifted one shoulder. "I should take care of any further issues myself, but thanks anyway." Reece made her feel stronger. He made her feel powerful.

"Well, keep me in mind. Because if I'd known that earlier, I could have 'accidentally' punched him in the throat before he left. Trust me, it would have been my pleasure."

She laughed. "I appreciate that, too. I'll let you know if he acts up again."

"You do that." He held her car key up. "I'll be back soon."

Jessica nodded. "I'll look forward to it."

"Maybe I can come up into the building and see where you work."

She shook her head. "I don't think so. You just want another opportunity to 'accidentally' punch Neil in the throat."

His eyebrows lifted and he laughed. "You're right. I guess I'm pretty obvious."

"Well, I'm a trained professional."

"With a sexy badge." He kissed her cheek.

"Damn straight." She placed a light kiss on his mouth. It was only a peck, but her lips tingled with pleasure all the same, along with another, more intimate, place in her body, making her anxious for tonight even if she had to share him with an FBI op.

Reece walked away whistling. She watched every step until he exited. He had a great butt, too. Head floating in the clouds, Jessica managed to get back to her desk without incident. The phone started ringing the moment she sat, as if someone watched her. She didn't recognize the number on the display.

"Agent Hayes," she said in as professional a voice as she could muster.

"Do you still have a date for tonight?" Pierce asked.

"Yes."

"Did you invite your long-lost college roommate and friend out dancing tonight?"

"Not yet. I figured it would play better as a really late addition. I didn't want him to decide to go somewhere else if the others were coming along."

There was silence on the other end of the line as if he assessed her reasoning for holes he could argue, but didn't. "All right then. Are you meeting him at the club?"

"No, he's coming to pick me up at my place. Elsa and Gordon can show up an hour before, but if you want to sell it, they better have luggage."

"This is not my first rodeo, Agent. That's already in the works."

The rodeo phrase he uttered in such a matter-of-fact way struck her as hilarious. She had to stifle a laugh, coughing to cover her amusement. But if he watched her from somewhere, he'd see her laughing at him. Hopefully her temporary boss had a sense of humor.

"Good. I assume you have my address already."

"Indeed, we do."

"Anything else I need to do at my house to prepare? Or any tasks I'll have to take care of once we're inside the club tonight?"

"No. You're providing the way inside and distracting your date to keep him from figuring out what your long-lost friends are doing."

"Oh? I have to distract him, too?" Jessica could only think of one singular thing that was certain to distract Reece, but it wasn't something she'd do in public.

There was silence at the end of the line again. "Well, yeah. Although, given how protective he is of you, I suspect you won't have to do anything you weren't planning to do anyway."

"How do you know he's protective of me?"

Another long silence ensued. In a low tone he asked, "Did you forget, Agent Hayes, that federal buildings have lots of video cameras recording twenty-four-seven, especially in the lobby? For a couple of seconds, I thought your guy might do us all a favor and take Wiley out permanently."

Jessica straightened her posture as if by reflex and looked over at the camera in the corner of the office. "I'm going to go out on a limb and assume you didn't send nimrod, I mean, Neil down to get me."

"Your assumption is correct. Besides, you already know he's off my team."

"Still? I figured he'd tattled to his uncle by now."

"Doesn't matter. I outrank his uncle. He's off permanently. If he ever bothers you again, I'll expect you to tell me. Your new boyfriend isn't the only one willing to punch that douche bag in the throat."

"You had audio, too?" Jessica felt the blood drain from her face. What else had she said to Reece? Good heavens above, had he heard them talking about her badge and Reece's discarded shirt? *Shit. Shit. Shit.*

"No comment. Keep in mind that I will be listening in tonight, as well. Elsa will give you a small communication device to tuck inside your ear, so you'll be kept abreast of our progress."

"Is that a good idea? I don't want Reece to see it." That would be a difficult thing to explain or she'd have to lie and say it was to enhance her non-existent hearing loss. Which he wouldn't believe, because how lame was that? She wouldn't believe it either. *Shit.*

"Don't worry, it's the latest tech and very small. You'll forget it's there."

That's what I'm worried about.

Jessica closed her eyes and hoped Reece wouldn't notice the device or nibble her ears as they danced. Or divulge anything of a personal nature that she didn't want the entire FBI to hear, which was ridiculous because they'd be dirty dancing in the middle of the floor as he whispered naughty things in her mic all night. "Awesome," she whispered to herself.

Pierce must have heard the sarcasm in her tone. "Listen, Agent Hayes, I know this isn't an ideal situation for you personally. I want you to know that I do appreciate your sacrifice. The recording tonight is for tactical reasons. Only a very limited list of people will ever hear what is said tonight. I hope that's helpful."

"It is. Thank you." *And even if it's not, I don't have much choice, do I?*

Pierce then added, "When he brings your car keys

back, ask him to pick you up around nine. That should give us plenty enough time to prepare."

"Got it."

Apparently Pierce was watching the parking lot video, too. Two hours later, he called to give her a heads up that Reece was back with her car. She was able to meet him in the lobby without being called down.

The minute he saw her standing where they'd been before, he smiled and approached her. "Did you set up surveillance on me or something?"

"Of course. That's what FBI agents with badges do all day. Didn't you know?"

He grinned. "Well, I had my suspicions." He handed her the key, but grabbed her hand and held on. "What is your address and what time can I pick you up tonight?"

"I'll text you my address. How about nine o'clock? I should be home and fairly presentable by then."

"Perfect. See you tonight." He strolled away, whistling a happy tune.

She'd wanted to kiss him, hug him and apologize in advance for tonight, but refrained from touching him at all, not trusting herself.

Jessica hoped tonight went smoothly, and that he never had any idea what was really about to happen at his exclusive club.

CHAPTER 8

While he sat in Tire Planet's waiting room waiting for Jessica's flat to be repaired, Reece sent a courtesy text to Hector, the bouncer on duty this evening at the Lexicon Club, that he'd be there with a date. Hector asked if it was the female Fed he'd been seen with in the media coverage after the coffee shop robbery.

Reece confirmed it, knowing Hector would pipe it immediately to the owner of the Lexicon Club. Travis Arthur owned a lot of clubs, but none more high-end and exclusive than the LC, which was his pride and joy.

Arthur didn't care for anyone in law enforcement invading or being involved with any of his clubs, especially not the LC, at least not until now. What he did like was the idea of having a pipeline into the inner workings of the FBI.

Reece was about to prove his worth and his willingness to play along with Arthur's rules. It had taken quite a long time to earn the trust of a man who didn't give it easily. Honestly, tonight would truly cement him into this organization where he might finally be able to see the end of his undercover work here.

Ideally, he wanted to get Arthur's sacred files. The man was the very definition of well connected. He knew everyone, and everyone knew him, from local guys to criminals all over the world. But no one seemed to know where Arthur kept his contact list. No one even knew what form the list was in. It could be a flashdrive in a safe, a little black book in his back pocket, or a hard copy ream of paper in a safety deposit box in Switzerland.

Through the LC grapevine, Arthur had learned about Reece and the coffee shop robbery and that subsequently Reece had been seen in the company of that same agent the next morning. It was even possible Arthur had a contact in the FBI already feeding him cursory information.

Reece hoped not. If Arthur was all gung-ho on the *go date a federal agent* track, he must not have the access he wanted. Arthur would be at the club tonight. He'd want to see Jessica for himself and meet her. Reece would have to be a lot more forward than he would normally be if they were just out on a date and his job wasn't dictating his actions.

Reece's one caveat to his undercover superiors was that any information fed into the LC grapevine to Arthur would not come from Jessica. They'd agreed when he pressed, although it didn't matter. Ultimately, they'd find some plausible excuse to force him to do exactly what they wanted, regardless of his wishes.

They always did.

Not for the first time, Reece contemplated giving up this life and trying something else for a change of pace. He loved the action and pretending to be someone else was a kick, but he was tired of it. After this job—if it ever ended—he planned to look around. His brother Zak was involved with a group called The Organization, doing similar but privately funded work, and he seemed to like it there. It was an option, anyway.

Reece just needed to hang tough for a little while

longer. Once he fully gained Arthur's trust, discovered where he kept his history and contact files and then appropriated them, he'd be free to leave this seemingly endless operation.

His only true regret when the time came would be leaving Jessica, if they were still together. He hoped privately they would still be a couple. Although, given the secrecy and sensitivity of this job—not to mention the expense of his lengthy stay here—he'd never be given permission to divulge any after-action info to her anyway. Reece might have to leave the area to go to another job in another city on the whim of his chain of command.

In fact, he might have to leave her without even saying goodbye. A depressing thought he tucked away as useless to worry about right now.

Reece parked his car near her apartment building and headed for her door. There was no security in her building beyond whatever personal locks she had on her door. He was able to go straight to her apartment on the second floor without being buzzed in.

Standing in the hallway outside her door, he thought he heard voices on the other side, but also heard music. Maybe she was getting her courage up for tonight.

He knocked twice and the door was swept open quickly, as if she'd been standing there waiting for him. When he saw her, all civil and logical thought drained from his head. She'd straightened her hair and wore it down. He liked her work look of a tidy ponytail, but her evening style was spectacular.

The outfit she wore, or rather almost wore, caught his attention next. He saw a low-cut neckline, lots of cleavage, and black leather. There were triangular inserts of dark red leather beneath her breasts, presumably to make them look bigger, which he liked, and more artfully placed red leather inserts along the lower hem of the top.

The skirt was extremely short. Next he noticed her bare thighs and the black leather boots that came above her knees. The question of what she was wearing beneath her skirt would be reserved for the dance floor, if he could talk her out there, or perhaps later this evening if he could talk her back to his place.

She did a little curtsy and asked, "What do you think?"

He leaned against the doorframe. "I think we should stay in tonight."

"Very funny. I'll have you know that I spent considerable time straightening my hair to get it to look this good. Trust me. We're going out."

He gave her a predatory grin. "Perfect."

"Also, I have another not-so perfect surprise." She glanced over her shoulder and then gestured him inside. There were two mismatched suitcases by the sofa in the living room and he heard voices beyond a door on the other side of the room.

"I have two unexpected guests."

"I see that." His gaze went to the door across the room again when laughter peeled from there.

"My semi-flaky, yet very lovable college roommate, Elsa, and her boyfriend Gordon surprised me less than an hour ago. They came for an impromptu visit."

"That's okay. Are we still going out?" He glanced at her hair again. "I mean, you did spend all that time on your hair, which looks amazing, by the way. Honestly, you look stunning."

"Thanks." She directed her gaze to the floor, pushed out a breath, shook her head and started talking. "The thing is, I told them where I was going tonight. They squealed in delight and immediately assumed they'd be able to go with us." Her gaze flitted to his face before dropping to the floor again. Her cheeks were pink.

"I see." She was adorable.

"I'll understand if it's a problem." From across the room, they both turned when another high-pitched squeal came from behind the closed door across the room. "I will, however, make *you* explain it to them."

Reece took her in his arms and kissed her. She tasted so fucking good. "It's not a problem, Smith. I'm just delighted we still have a date. I may have mentioned to my co-workers that I was bringing someone to the club tonight. Doesn't matter how many of us show up as long as you do."

"Are you sure? I'm not a club girl, as I mentioned, but Elsa most definitely is. The two of them had actually *heard* of your club. I mean, they *really* want to go with us tonight. I hope that's not an issue."

Reece winked. "No worries. I can get us all in." In fact, that would be perfect for his needs tonight. Instead of awkwardly introducing her around the club, he could play host and do it while impressing her out-of-town friends, and while he romanced her publically through the night with all eyes in the club watching them canoodle.

Just then the door across the room burst open and a girl and a guy ambled out, dressed in club clothing and seemingly ready to party all night. By her name, he'd expected Elsa to be a tall, ice-blonde Swedish girl, but she was tiny and brunette. He'd thought Gordon would be a mid-western farm boy, but he was an Asian dude who looked totally in love with his woman. Often stereotypes didn't work for names, as in this case.

Jessica made quick introductions. Elsa and Gordon were enthusiastic about being able to dance the night away in to the famous Lexicon Club. After a very brief discussion, where Reece formally invited them to the club, they all were headed out the door. He drove, since he could get premium parking. The four of them walked past the very long line of people on the way to the corner door.

"Are you sure it's okay that we're passing all these people by?"

Was Jessica expecting booing and hissing from the crowd? She had both hands wrapped around one of his biceps as they made their way to the door.

"Don't worry. This is just the way it works," he told her. In fact, many of the people waiting recognized Reece and waved at him. Reece glanced down at her sexy outfit again. If he hadn't already met her, he would have certainly allowed her access to the club. He nodded to several well-dressed patrons as he passed by them in line before making it to where Hector stood guard. The bouncer gave Jessica a subtle once over as they approached. Hector must have approved, since he gave them a rare smile.

Tonight was a weeknight, but at this club it didn't seem to matter. Every night was busy. Reece leaned in and said in a low voice that his girl had unexpected out-of-town guests and they'd wanted to come along. Hector only nodded and gave him a knowing look. Lots of people wanted to get inside. Few had automatic access like he did.

Hector unhooked the velvet rope and allowed all four of them entrance without further question or conversation. Reece was relieved, even though he knew he'd be allowed inside regardless of the number of folks he brought along. Not to mention that Arthur had invited him and his new FBI girlfriend specifically.

The moment he opened the door to the club, loud music poured past them and into the street. The three entered the song-filled fray and he followed them inside. The host, Sam, who handled the premium seating in the club, saw Reece and waved him over to the booth to the right of the entry.

"Reece. I heard you had a special guest tonight, bro, so I reserved a table in the exclusive area for you."

"Really? Thanks. Will it seat four? My date had surprise guests this evening so we brought them along."

"Of course. Nothing but the best for you. As a matter of fact, I've got you center court."

Center court meant the best table in the house. Arthur had gone all out. They'd even have a private waiter taking care of their complimentary food and drink orders. It also meant that Reece wouldn't have to find Arthur, he'd find them now that he'd put them center court in the club. Everyone in attendance would see them. That could be good or bad.

Reece pretended everything was going to be good.

"Thanks, Sam."

"Need an escort?"

"Nope. I can do it." Reece guided Jessica and her friends to the premium area, hoping tonight would go as smooth as his Jessica's lovely hair.

The best seat in the place was half a story up in the middle of the club with a private entrance to the dance floor. They walked up an exclusive wide ramp that wound upward along the edge of the vast dance floor to the oversized, horseshoe-shaped table on its own platform.

A decorative cascade of wide steps on the other side of the platform offered direct access to the dance floor. If one walked further along the ramp, they'd come to several more premium tables situated facing the dancers, also with access to the private bar servicing them. However, any needs of this premium table were met first and foremost by the exclusive bartender.

"Order whatever you want tonight, my treat. It isn't often I get to use this perk, so enjoy."

Elsa and Gordon oohed and ahhed, suitably impressed with the club in general and especially the premium table and open bar, thanking Reece repeatedly for allowing them to come along tonight.

They'd barely gotten seated before the waiter asked for their drink orders. Jessica's friends ordered top-shelf stuff and then folded into each other, soon dancing their way to the edge of the main dance floor.

It wasn't long before the owner made his way over, with his ever-present bodyguard in tow. Arthur didn't have much patience when he had an agenda. He did make a big show of it, though, strolling up to the table with arms open wide like they were long-lost relatives reunited once again. His personal assistant and bodyguard, Dixon, stood back a couple of paces to let his boss work. "Reece, it's so good to see you here on your night off."

Reece stood and shook hands with Arthur to add credence to the show, hoping he wouldn't have to give him hugs and kisses, as well. One big happy crime family was on the menu for this evening's entertainment, but it didn't mean they had to get fake physical, in his opinion.

"Who do you have with you tonight?" Arthur leaned down to Jessica, raising his voice to be heard over the thumping beat of the music.

Reece played his part. "Arthur, this is my good friend, Jessica. She's the one I told you about. Jessica, this is the Lexicon Club's owner and my boss, Travis Arthur."

Arthur looked genuinely happy when he extended a hand to her. "So good to meet you, Jessica. It's exceedingly rare that Reece brings anyone to our club. In fact, I don't remember the last time. You must be very special."

Jessica smiled and shook his hand. "Thank you. I'm pleased to meet you, as well. Your club is beautiful."

Arthur nodded, glancing over one shoulder with utter pride coating his expression. He was very proud of himself and his stellar place of business. "It is my favorite of them all. Have a wonderful time here tonight."

"I will."

Reece breathed a sigh of relief. He was afraid she'd be given twenty questions regarding her profession. Then again, his boss wasn't foolish. He played along. He never made anyone feel uncomfortable. That was likely why he had so many important contacts. Arthur knew how to cultivate and keep them. Reece just wished he knew the method used.

Jessica would be categorized as his government girlfriend, filed away, and then trotted out for use at some future date when Arthur needed a favor. Reece hoped he'd be out of this business well before Jessica was ever brought up again. However, it might be wishful thinking on his part.

Arthur started to walk away. Reece was about sit and get down to serious canoodling when Arthur's bodyguard, Dixon, suddenly put his hand up to his ear as if someone was speaking or directing him. And it wasn't Arthur. Dixon glanced around the room as if by reflex, but apparently didn't see anything out of line.

The entire staff always had earpieces in place during work hours in case extra hands were needed to get rid of an unruly customer. Sometimes all they'd hear was a location repeated. Like trauma workers headed to a code for a patient in distress, workers not otherwise engaged would migrate to the troubled area.

Reece wasn't wearing his earpiece right now because it was his night off, although he'd certainly help out if needed.

It was one big happy crime family, after all.

Jessica caught his attention when she leaned back in her chair, looking out at the dance floor where her friends danced wildly in the crowd. They were also sliding erotically all over each other. She still seemed worried about them coming along. Meanwhile, Reece was grateful.

The raucous song filled with not so subtle innuendo came to an end and they stopped dancing a few moments later. Elsa and Gordon kissed enthusiastically as a new song began, but started making their way back to the booth. Perhaps they needed refreshments. Or a private room.

Dixon whispered something in Arthur's ear. Reece could have sworn he heard, "FBI agent." Was Dixon talking about Jessica? Arthur turned toward the front of the club, as did his bodyguard. Dixon put himself half a step ahead of Arthur.

Reece looked at the front door. Jessica's nemesis, Agent Neil Wiley, stood just inside the doorway. He wore a determined expression as he searched the room with a disdain-filled stare.

CHAPTER 9

"What in the ever-loving *fuck* is Wiley doing at the Lexicon Club?" Jessica heard Pierce's question blaze in her tiny earpiece, but managed to remain calm. She deserved an award for not acknowledging the voice or leaping out of the booth in shock when she heard Neil's name.

She'd managed to get through the difficult chore of meeting Travis Arthur, the club's owner and Reece's boss, only to hear that Neil was outside the club. Nothing like sneaking in to plant bugs and trying to maintain a nonchalant attitude when vocal alarms were going off in her head predicting impending doom, all while pretending she was only here on a date.

Pierce, currently stationed in the mobile surveillance van somewhere nearby with Seth, was the first to see Neil approach the bouncer on duty. He gave a play-by-play of the events outside the club.

In a low, tight voice that could not be mistaken for anything but seething anger, Pierce said, "Did that dumbass prick just flash his badge to get inside this club? I am going to hurt him. I will tear him limb from limb."

Apparently, Hector the bouncer wasn't happy, but let

Neil in all the same. This made Pierce's voice rise to an even higher octave, making clear his further disapproval over her wide-open communication line when Neil was ushered through the front entrance.

"Fuck. Why are you letting him in, *Other* Bouncer Guy? It's your job is to keep out the riffraff, isn't it?" Pierce asked those last questions before apparently realizing he'd been shouting over the open channel.

From the dance floor, Gordon said, "Looks like they've notified the bodyguard standing with the owner. Everyone at the target table is looking over at the front door where he's standing."

Elsa asked, "What do you want us to do? Intercept him?"

"No," Pierce said. "Go back to the table. Do what you need to do. Maybe if he sees the three of you together he'll get a clue and back the fuck off."

Jessica disagreed. *I wouldn't be so sure. Neil isn't known for having a clue.* She didn't think it was a sound plan, but she was unable to comment on the current conversation playing out in her ear.

"I'll send Seth in," Pierce said in a more normal tone. "He will shove Neil outside again before that idiot sees anyone, makes a big stink about it, and fucks this mission up any more than he already has."

"What?" Seth asked in a loud tone. She'd be deaf by the end of the night if this drama kept up.

Pierce whispered instructions to Seth and then it sounded like he fairly kicked him out of the surveillance van with a loose plan for getting Neil out of the club. Meanwhile, Jessica watched Elsa and Gordon kiss exuberantly after their wild erotic dance ended.

Were they a couple? She hadn't gotten that vibe at all until they'd exited her bedroom when Reece arrived. Maybe it was all for show. But if they weren't together, they were amazing at undercover work.

Jessica was a foolish novice by comparison. Pierce hadn't directed her to do anything, so she tried to just stay in the moment of *I'm at an exclusive club with my new awesome guy*. But with Neil about to cause mayhem with his unwanted presence, it was difficult to concentrate on anything but being found out or embarrassed or both.

She almost startled again when Reece said to his boss, "Don't worry. I'll take care of this." He put his hand gently on Jessica's shoulder and said, "Do you think he followed us here because of what happened earlier today?"

She opened her mouth to say no, because she knew very well how Neil knew about this place. It had been in the briefing before the moron had gotten himself thrown out for being inappropriate with her.

She thought better of it and shrugged. "I wouldn't put it past him, but I don't know that for certain. I've only dealt with him at work. He did see you today, though, and unfortunately he does have access to the same information I do as far as looking people up."

"Okay." Reece winked and her heart skipped a beat. "I'm going to go get rid of him. If he doesn't have a warrant, I'll ask him to wait outside."

Pierce said, "Is it ironic to anyone else that one of the guys we've got under surveillance is about to save our collective asses from one of our own fucking agents?"

Jessica ignored Pierce's remark, smiled at Reece and said, "Fine. Just don't punch him in the throat."

In her earpiece, Pierce muttered, "No. Please punch him hard. Put him out of my misery."

"No promises," Reece said, dropping a kiss on her knuckles.

Arthur, Reece and the bodyguard had a brief discussion before Reece nodded once and strode away to take care of business. Jessica had a direct line of sight as Reece approached the entrance. She wanted to hide under the table and hope Neil didn't see her. She worried that if he saw her, he'd be an even bigger prick and more difficult to get rid of.

Jessica wished she could listen in on their conversation. Her wish was granted. As Reece got within six feet of Neil, Seth—and his earpiece—came through the front entrance.

Seth, looking extremely uncomfortable, said, "Neil, buddy, we aren't meeting at this club. Come on. Let's go. I've got a car waiting outside."

Neil the Idiot looked totally surprised to see Seth. He said loudly, "What are you doing here?" Jessica was amazed he didn't call out Seth's full title and name, then identify him as an undercover FBI agent currently on an operation.

Reece joined the two seconds later. "Sorry, dude. Unless you have a warrant, we reserve the right to refuse service to anyone. You'll have to go."

"I have every right to be here." Neil puffed his chest out and glared at Reece.

"Not if you used your badge to gain entrance," Reece said in a calmer tone than she would have used. "Badge plus warrant equals entrance. Nothing else works in this situation. You should know that."

"He's right," Pierce remarked tersely. "Seth, grab that moronic asshole and haul him outside right now. I've got a government vehicle on its way to you at the front door. Get him inside it, pronto."

Seth did as he was told. He grabbed Neil's arm and pulled him toward the door. Neil yanked his arm away. Straightening his clothes, he tried to head back into the club. Reece body-blocked him, shoved him toward the door and all three men went to the front entrance together. Seth pulled, Reece pushed, and Neil fought all the way out the front door, swearing a blue streak that would make a biker blush.

Elsa and Gordon sat down at the table with Jessica. Arthur stood only a few paces away, his bodyguard stationed beside him. They picked up their drinks and sipped, talking animatedly about how great the place was and how glad they were that Jessica had invited them, seemingly oblivious to the drama happening at the front door.

Arthur and his bodyguard moved away. Reece was obviously trusted to take care of this issue even though it was his night off. Jessica looked hard at Dixon's face before he retreated, feeling like she'd seen him before. He seemed vaguely familiar but she couldn't place him.

She was usually good at identifying people. Some people were good at numbers. Others were good at remembering names. She was good at facial recognition but blamed the stress of the evening on her inability in this moment. Eventually it would come to her.

Jessica tried not to look nervous as Elsa and Gordon implemented their plan to place bugs at the premium table. It was some luck they got seated here instead of trying to find a way to crash this table as drunk, loud dance revelers. Elsa opened her purse, extracted a pocket mirror and her lip-gloss, and made a show of putting a new coat on, all the while keeping up a happy conversation with Gordon and Jessica. Her date was busy fastening state of the art listening devices beneath the table.

Outside, the battle continued as Jessica listened through Seth's mic. Neil was affronted. "You may be the head bouncer here, but you aren't such hot shit. I could bring you down if I wanted—"

There was happy chatter in one ear and idiotic chatter in her other. It was enough to give her a blinding headache.

Elsa and Gordon looked at her, rolling their eyes, presumably at Neil's bad behavior. Elsa whispered, "I almost feel sorry for him." *I don't.* Karma was a bitch, and in Neil's case it was long overdue in coming around to bite him in the ass.

Jessica heard tires squeal in the background noise of her earpiece.

Seth said, "Come on, Neil. Here's our ride. Let's go."

"I'm not ready to leave."

Reece said, "You are not getting back into the club, dude. Say goodnight."

Gaining a bit of bravado, possibly because he was out of the club and Pierce continued to bark in all their ears, Seth said, "Neil, get in this vehicle right now! I mean it!"

There were sounds of a scuffle, like Seth was getting physical with Neil. Jessica wished she had a visual of it. Reece said to Seth, "Thanks, man. I appreciate the help."

"No problem." A door slammed. There was another squeal of tires.

Neil was yelling something, but his words weren't distinguishable.

Seth finally said, "You prick, you almost blew our whole operation."

"Operation? Was something going on inside there tonight?"

Pierce said, "Don't give him any more information, Seth. The vehicle is on the way to my location. Gordon. Elsa. Do what we planned. Don't forget the bathrooms."

Jessica watched the front door as Pierce gave his instructions. Reece came through a couple of seconds later and headed in their direction. Jessica said, "Reece is on his way back to our table."

Pierce said, "Let's just go with the idea that Neil got illegal info on where your boyfriend worked and came in because of what happened in the lobby earlier today."

"Got it," Jessica said in a low tone, and smiled as Reece slid into the booth beside her.

"Disaster averted," he said, picking up his drink and taking a healthy slug.

"Is his throat region intact?" she asked, putting her hand on his thigh beneath the table.

"This time it is, but no promises for next time."

"Everything okay?" Elsa asked.

"It is now," Jessica said. "I'll tell you all about it later." Reece put his palm over her hand, the one still resting on his thigh. He pressed down and squeezed her fingers, keeping her trapped there. It wasn't like she'd planned to desert him.

Their dedicated waiter brought them a second round of drinks along with complimentary appetizers, probably to make them thirsty, but it didn't matter because Reece was picking up the tab for this extravagant evening. That bothered her.

In her ear she heard Pierce saying he was signing off for a few minutes to deal with Neil. *Oh, to be a fly on the wall during* that *meeting.* Seth remained on the line for tactical information and to report any further disturbances from outside the club. Jessica guessed it was too much to hope that Pierce would get rid of Neil forever. Hadn't she seen a posting in northern Alaska advertised recently?

Seconds later, the DJ told the room he was slowing things down for all those lovers out there who wanted to snuggle. Reece said, "That's our cue. Come and dance with me. Don't worry, we'll just sway back and forth. I'll lead."

Jessica scooted out of the booth. "Did you bribe the DJ to play slow music just to get me out on the dance floor?"

"Of course. That's what bouncers with hot dates do all night. Didn't you know?"

She laughed, remembering she'd said something similar when they were on her turf in the lobby of the Federal Building.

Elsa and Gordon elected to stay at the booth and snuggle there instead, saying they preferred fast music while out on the dance floor.

True to his word, Reece took her in his arms. He put his face at her temple after kissing her cheek gently. They soon swayed deliciously to soft music. There were quite a few other couples dancing, but she barely noticed them, doing her best to ignore the occasional voice in her ear from others on the team.

Jessica worried he might hear it if Pierce started screaming again. In the lessons learned portion of their debriefing tomorrow, she'd mention her fears in that regard as a tip moving forward.

Elsa and Gordon took turns in the men's and women's on-site facilities, planting their listening devices in inconspicuous places. For now Jessica did her best to ignore any random conversation buzzing in her ear to focus on the seriously hot guy dancing her around the room. She'd always hated dancing, but she loved swaying in Reece's arms. Perhaps at long last she'd found the right partner.

"Thanks for getting rid of Neil," she said. "I'm sorry he came here tonight."

"No worries. I didn't do much except get him outside. His friend was the one who hustled him into a waiting vehicle the moment we got out there. Come to think of it, that car showing up when it did was really great timing."

Jessica didn't say anything, but the hairs on the back of her neck stood at attention. She didn't want him thinking through who picked Neil up. She kissed his neck in a place she knew was sensitive, trying to distract him from his current thought process. It wasn't exactly a chore, but she felt like she was using him as she did it.

He started to make a sound, clearing his throat instead, but she liked that she had some sensual power over him. She licked the spot she'd just kissed, eliciting another low growl of approval. Reece responded in kind, first pressing his lips to her brow, then trailing sweet kisses down her face.

When he got near her mouth, he kissed her lips like they were all alone. His fingertips skimmed along her spine headed for her ass. He pressed his hand in the center, pulling her lower half closer. He broke the kiss, staring at her much like he had the night they'd met. Like he was hungry. Like he wanted to do wild things to her.

She wanted to grant him complete access.

Reece gave her that special half smile he had when he was amused. She liked it. She wanted him. She wondered where they'd end up tonight or even *if* they'd end up together.

Jessica had fake overnight guests to contend with who weren't really spending the night, but she couldn't very well tell him that. Or she could usher him into her bedroom and put Elsa and Gordon on her pull-out sofa, but then they'd have to listen to her and Reece satisfying their hunger for each other all night long.

Jessica wanted to go home with the hot, sexy bouncer who liquefied her insides with a mere kiss, but figured she'd likely end up sleeping alone.

For the first time all night, she startled when Pierce came back on her earpiece, asking Elsa and Gordon about their progress. He hadn't even shouted.

Reece looked down at her. "Are you okay?"

She nodded, but didn't look at him, feeling her cheeks warming up.

"What's wrong?"

She wanted to say nothing, but felt obligated to

respond. "I feel bad saying this, but I wish I didn't have guests tonight."

"Oh?"

Jessica looked into his eyes and said, "Actually, I'd rather *you* were the only guest in my apartment tonight."

There was sudden silence on her earpiece. No one said a word.

He smiled at her. "Me too. But I understand."

She really did wish it, but felt a sudden rash of guilt over using him the way she was tonight, especially after all he'd done for her, both the things he knew about and the things he didn't.

Did the guilt show on her face? She hoped not. He gave her an odd look, but then pulled her tightly into his arms as they continued swaying to the music. His scent. His warmth. His body. All combined to make her wish they'd met in such a way that he wasn't part of her job.

Guilt was a heavy burden, eating away at her very soul. She probably wouldn't sleep a wink tonight no matter whose bed she ended up in.

As the slow music wound down, Reece whispered in her ear, "Tell me something. Did Neil really follow us here tonight or is something else going on?"

Jessica stiffened, pulling away before she could consciously stop herself. They parted enough that he was looking at her. She knew she must look guilty.

Her mouth opened and then closed. She shook her head as her eyes welled with tears.

Reece's eyes widened as he stared into hers. "Wait. Do you have *me* under surveillance?"

CHAPTER 10

The incident with Neil and the unusual way he'd been removed from the premises hit Reece like a blow to his breadbasket. How many times had he seen that actual takedown in tactical security seminars over his career? Twenty? More? But then instead of being cool and pondering the possibilities in his head, he blurted out accusatory questions like a first-year recruit.

Given his background, he should have guessed sooner what might be going on. Jessica sidelined his brain, but that wasn't her fault. It was possible she didn't have impulsive guests with a burning desire to access to his exclusive club for secret FBI purposes, but he doubted it.

The truth of the situation rested in her current guilt-filled expression.

"I...don't have you under surveillance." The brief pause was a giveaway. She was lying.

"I don't believe you," he said, hearing the shock in his own voice. It was a knee-jerk reaction because he was so surprised. Truthfully, anything she said would have astounded him.

It wasn't so much Neil showing up as the way his nerdy-looking friend got him out and into the back of a waiting sedan with darkened windows and government tags. How had that been planned so well, unless the car had already been standing by?

Reece figured there was likely a communications van located somewhere close by with a live visual on the club. They saw Neil come in, went bat-shit crazy and had him hauled out.

Jessica turned away, moving out of his arms half a step. Not good. Was she mad at him? Was he mad at her? Yes. Maybe. No. Not really. He needed to figure his next step out quickly and act accordingly. No need to ruin this evening with bullshit from either of their work lives. In fact, even if she was lying her ass off to him tonight, she didn't know who he really was either, so he'd been just as deceitful.

If she or her chain of command was running an operation—and they probably were—he didn't care. It didn't change much as far as his circumstances were concerned. Arthur was happy because he supposedly had an FBI agent available for consultation on matters for his club, even though Reece wasn't going to actually feed him any legitimate information from Jessica. If her people were doing a surveillance operation, he should try to help them.

The slow music came to an end and a fast-beat tune started up. Jessica slowly headed off the dance floor. He let her get five steps away while he tried to calculate the best way to repair this foolishness. His feet started moving before he even knew what he'd say. When he got next to her, she didn't so much hang her head as refuse to look him in the eye for the rest of the trip back to the table.

He walked silently for a few more steps before crowding behind her and stopping her at the edge of the cascade of stairs. He grabbed her and buried his face against her ear. "I'm sorry, Jessica. Please forgive me. I shouldn't have said that. I know you aren't having me surveilled. Your stupid work stalker showing up here surprised me, and I reacted poorly." He hugged her hard to convey his sincerity.

She relaxed. "Well, I'm sorry Neil is such a prick. This little fight between us is one more reason to kick his sorry ass when I get back to work tomorrow."

"Wait. What? We aren't fighting, are we?" *Please say no.* He forced himself to chill and kissed the back of her neck.

She turned in his arms and hugged him tight, pushing her face against his throat, her lips pressing into a particular special place that put his mind elsewhere every time she kissed him there.

"Not anymore," she said, kissing him again. "Certainly not because of him."

Elsa and Gordon brushed past them on their way out to the dance floor.

Reece made a point of following her companions with his gaze and said quietly, "So I guess make-up sex is out of the question tonight, right?"

Jessica smiled. "Well, my apartment is really small."

He shrugged. "And?"

"Unless you have a proclivity for others listening in while we are together intimately, I'm going with *out of the question.*"

Reece tilted his head to one side. "Not personally a fan of performing to more than a crowd of one other person in the vicinity."

"Yeah, me neither. I also hate it when others are listening into my personal conversations."

He nodded. "I'm so glad we agree on these points."

She pushed out a frustrated-sounding sigh. "Unfortunately, that also means make-up sex is out of the question tonight."

"You could come home with me." He couldn't get

the vision out of his head of her naked, willing and wrapped in his arms for the rest of the night.

"Definitely tempting. If only it didn't put me in the category of worst hostess of the year."

Reece glanced out at the couple dirty dancing, wondering if Jessica would be listening to *them* go at it until dawn or exhaustion set in. His next thought was a vision of being snuggled up behind Jessica in her bed while they both pretended to sleep, but listened to Elsa and Gordon all night long. He didn't want anyone to watch *him* have sex, but the reverse wasn't true, and listening in was a close second to watching.

Jessica kissed his jaw, drawing his attention to where it should be. He pressed his lips to hers. "My back seat is an option once we drop them off at your place and shove them out of the car." He waggled his eyebrows.

She laughed. "I love how you don't give up so easily."

"Well, I *really* want to make up with you."

She pressed her soft lips to his chin. "Me, too. So raincheck, yes?"

"Yes. And soon."

"Definitely soon."

They went back to their premium table, sipped their drinks, held hands and kissed at every opportunity. He tried to initiate a more intimate chat once they were alone, but if he talked about anything too personal, she'd look like she wanted to speak, but ultimately backed out of the discussion and changed the subject to less volatile topics. It took him an hour to realize she was likely wired and someone was listening in on their conversation.

Not wanting to make her any more uncomfortable than she already was, Reece changed tactics and talked all about himself. Well, he discussed his fake background, which did not include four brothers. Luckily, she never brought up the slip he'd made at the FBI building regarding his four brothers.

By the time they left at midnight, she knew every well-orchestrated lie in his bogus backstory. Pleading general fatigue and work the next day, Jessica told Elsa and Gordon she needed to leave. If they wanted to stay, they'd have to get a taxi home.

Reece perked up briefly, explaining that they were welcome to stay until the club closed at two in the morning, but they opted to leave with him and Jessica. He drove to her place and parked in a visitor's spot close to her building. Elsa and Gordon scurried out of the vehicle, giving repeated thanks for the amazing evening, and best of all leaving them alone in his car. She'd given Elsa a spare key earlier in case they got separated.

"Thank you so much for tonight." Jessica gave him a look like she wanted to devour him whole. He so wanted to help her.

"It was my pleasure. Your friends are nice."

Jessica smiled, released her seatbelt, and turned slowly to face him. Then she moved close and kissed him like they might never see each other again. He returned the lip lock, moving his seat all the way back to give them more room to embrace and to do the whole goodnight kiss the right way.

The kissing led to touching, he couldn't seem to help himself. After several minutes of heavy breathing that he hoped no one else was listening to, one thing led to another. Before long he'd pulled her over the center console to straddle his lap. Her miniskirt went dangerously high, revealing the skimpy thong undies she wore.

She kissed him hard and thoroughly. He loved it. Only barely thinking clearly, his hand moved along her inner thigh, seeking to pleasure her. Her flimsy panties were no match for his deft fingers, and once he got his thumb against her most sensitive spot, he rubbed, hoping to *relax* her at the very least before she left his car. Then maybe listening to Elsa and Gordon all night wouldn't be so torturous.

Jessica broke their kiss, sucked in a sharp, sexy breath, and stared deeply into his eyes, whispering, "So good," over and over as he touched her. Then she fastened her lips to his and drove her tongue inside his mouth to tangle deliciously. He stroked harder and faster beneath her miniskirt. "Don't stop," she whispered urgently. *I won't. Not until I hear you come.*

He was blatantly rigid beneath the fly of his trousers, and patently ignoring his libido. He concentrated so hard on kissing her and stroking her he didn't realize she'd unfastened his pants until he felt her hand grip his cock. He moaned the moment her fingers brushed his flesh.

She worked quickly, not only getting him freed from his boxers in a flash, but also impaling herself on his stiff cock before he could stop her. Would he have stopped her? No. He would not.

One hand went to her bare ass to help with leverage as she moved up and down. She'd shoved her miniskirt to her waist when they started kissing. The kiss hadn't ever broken as they connected fully. Reece pushed his hips upward as she rode him.

Five thrusts in, she moaned, the sound making him smile inside. She whispered, "Harder. Faster."

He obliged, speeding his movements, feeling the exact second she climaxed when her inner walls pulsed repeatedly around his dick. She broke the kiss, arching her back, and pointing her face to the roof of his car, making sexy sounds as she came.

Reece lasted one more deep stroke before the orgasm of a lifetime spewed from him like a volcano erupting. He grunted like a caveman, with about as much finesse, clutching her to him in a death squeeze as the powerful sensation of his release eventually subsided.

"Best make-up sex ever," he whispered against her chest, her leather shirt soft but sturdy against his face, her rapid heartbeat thudding against his ear.

"Yes," she said, ruffling the hair over his brow. He sucked in a deep breath, smelling her perfume, the leather of her shirt and her climax comingling together. She still breathed hard, but kissed his temple and hugged him as hard as he embraced her. As the warmth of their union registered, it was then he realized they hadn't used a condom.

The car windows around them were steamed opaque, but Jessica didn't care. He'd mentioned make-up sex earlier and she'd thought of nothing else for the rest of the night. She was not sorry. The make-up sex in his car had been worth the risk of any possible discovery. Thankfully, she didn't think any degenerate neighbors had watched them from the sidewalk and no police officer had knocked on the window with the butt of a flashlight, catching them in flagrante. As far as she was concerned, they'd gotten away with it.

As post-bliss sanity returned, she *was* sorry she hadn't remembered to ask him to put a condom in place. She'd ripped his clothes from him and embedded him within her body before he could deny or stay her desires. Did he have protection in his wallet? She didn't know. It hadn't even once occurred to her to ask until this moment, which was far too late. She was an idiot, a well-satisfied idiot, but an idiot nonetheless.

Reece cleared his throat, released her from the constricting hug he'd given her, and grabbed a square tissue box from his back seat. He handed it to her with a contrite look in his eyes. He might not have remembered either in the moment, but she blamed herself, not him.

She was the one who'd pulled his pants open and impaled herself before he seemed to realize her intent. He'd been about to make her come and she wanted to feel him deeply inside. She'd taken what she wanted regardless of the consequences, and vowed to never make him suffer for her spontaneous decision.

"I'm not sorry," she whispered, looking directly into his soulfully beautiful eyes. Even the image of being nine months pregnant and waddling up the front walkway of her childhood home unmarried and unemployed as her parents watched with her four older brothers lined up behind them on the porch didn't conjure any remorse.

"I'm not either. That felt way too good for any regrets." He grinned, winked and kissed her cheek. She disengaged, used several tissues to clean up, and settled back in the passenger seat to think about what had just happened. By the time she'd finished, he'd done the same and zipped his pants up.

"I hope you still feel that way tomorrow," she said quietly.

"Oh, trust me, I will. No worries." He grabbed her hand and kissed her knuckles. "I hope you also harbor no regrets by dawn's early light." His gaze traveled past her and out her steamed-up window. "Listen, I have to work the next five days, six at night until three in the morning. When will I see you again?"

Jessica pushed out a sigh, grateful they weren't going to discuss the consequences of her actions at this time. "Probably not until your next day off. I rarely get home until seven or eight at night."

"Lunch?"

"Infrequent and never at the exact same time."

"I can text you and leave messages on your phone though, right?"

"Sure." She looked toward her building with little

enthusiasm. "Guess I better get upstairs and get started on that hostess of the year award."

She reached for the door handle, but he wouldn't let go of her other hand. "Hang tight." He released her fingers, then popped open his door and came around to her side of the car as she exited.

Reece closed her door, laced their fingers together and started walking toward her building. Before she could even open her mouth to ask what he was doing, he said, "Yes. I *am* planning to walk you all the way to your doorstep. That's where I collected you earlier for our date. You aren't going to fight me on this, are you?" His signature sexy grin added to his charm. He pulled on her hand and she started moving again. Slowly.

Jessica wasn't certain if she should let him take her to her door. She didn't know where Elsa and Gordon were or what they were doing. "If I do, it's only because the make-up sex is so phenomenal."

She didn't stop him until they'd travelled through the lobby and stood before the central stairs leading to the next floor.

"Keep moving," he said, putting a foot on the first step.

"Will you be coming inside?"

His brows furrowed. "No. Not unless you want me to."

"Oh. I want you to. I thought I'd made that blatantly clear downstairs in the front seat of your car."

"So is this about you not trusting yourself to keep me out?"

"Maybe. I do have skills, you know." She smiled, stroking her fingers along his jaw. "I could get you inside my bedroom if I wanted to, and trust me, I do."

He grinned that oh-so-charming smile. "If I swear on all I hold sacred that I will *not* cross the threshold of your domain tonight, can we keep going?"

Leaning close, she whispered in his ear, "Sure. But what if I tempt you?"

"You already do."

"What if I promise to show you my FBI badge?" She flattened her palm against his chest, smoothing out the fabric. She then fingered the lapel of his shirt, toying with the first button a few inches below his collarbone. She slipped the button through the hole. He laughed, a low sound of dark amusement that made her heart skip a beat.

"Wow. You *do* have skills." He pressed against her, tangling his legs into hers and taking a couple of steps until she fell backward against the wall by the railing, practically clinging to him by the time they got there.

He planted his lips on hers hungrily. The kiss was devastating to every single one of her senses. She was overwhelmed in seconds, ready to go the distance. When she reached for his belt, he stopped her, wrapping his fingers around her hand and kissing the palm before placing it at her side forcefully.

Pulling back to stare affectionately into her face, he asked, "So, can I finish walking you upstairs now?" He didn't seem the least impacted by the kiss, while she was ready to melt in a puddle of need.

She laughed. "Great deflection. You have skills, too. Fine. Let's go."

"You don't even know how much it costs me to deny you, but I will if I must, this time. Just keep in mind that *next* time you might not be so lucky."

"Oh, I suspect I'm lucky either way."

Together they climbed to the second story and walked hand in hand to her door. He kissed her passionately before she unlocked her apartment.

As promised, he didn't try to get inside. Instead, he kissed her again. It was a sweet kiss, filled with promise and a hint of fire, but then it ended and he said goodnight, backing away with a satisfied expression on his face. She likely had an equally satisfied look.

Once her door was closed, she pushed out a long sigh, turned and startled when Elsa entered from the kitchen.

"He didn't come in?"

"No. We were exceptionally lucky already tonight. I didn't know what you two were doing. I didn't want to take any more chances. And I didn't want to push my luck any further either."

Elsa smiled like she wasn't sure she understood. "We were prepared."

"I wasn't."

"Oh? I don't know about that. You looked like you had things well in hand downstairs."

A rush of heat consumed her face. "You spied on me?"

She shrugged. "Perhaps I was worried when you were down in the car for so long."

"And will you be sharing your insight with the team tomorrow?"

"Of course not. That was private."

"Not as private as I initially thought," she muttered.

Elsa crossed the room, but then stopped halfway. "If I were you, I'd be more worried about whether Pierce turned the coms off after we left the club. I took my piece out of my ear and so did Gordon. Eventually." One eyebrow went up nearly to her hairline as Jessica's heart plummeted to her belly. She reached up and yanked the communication device from her ear. Elsa cleared her throat loudly and held her palm out for the earpiece before Jessica could hurl the forgotten device across the room.

She sucked in a deep breath to calm her racing heart, and pushed it out slowly. It was really just too much. She would either run screaming or break out into hysterical laugher, unable to stop at will.

Elsa put a hand on her shoulder. "Don't worry. Even if there is a recording, Pierce will ensure it's deleted. Okay?"

Jessica nodded.

"If I say please, will you make sure it's deleted either way? I don't have the nerve to ask Agent Pierce myself."

Elsa laughed. "That's not true, *chica*. You have plenty of nerve. And you did a great job tonight. But I'll make sure for you."

Jessica nodded. "Thank you." Now the only thing to worry about was a possible unexpected pregnancy. Well, that *and* if her brothers would promptly pull out a shotgun—or four of them—and beat the shit out of the only man she'd ever been in love with to force him into a hasty marriage.

CHAPTER 11

Several nights after the amazing make-up sex in his car, Reece was still thinking about it, and Jessica, and how he could make his relationship with her permanent even after this deep cover assignment was finished.

If there were ever any consequences to that sublime connection, he was fully ready to step up. She'd mentioned having four older brothers, which might be awkward, but she was worth any grief from anyone else. If he were smart he'd change jobs and pursue her. He'd have no problem with her career in the FBI. Who better than a current or former law enforcement officer to support her vocation?

Reece had enjoyed being undercover for the last ten years, but it was often lonely work. Circulating throughout the club this evening, ensuring everyone played nice, he contemplated his life *after* a long undercover role. One of his security instructors had once told him, "When you're ready to get out of the field, you'll know it in your gut."

Reece thought maybe his gut finally had something to say. Or maybe it was his cock doing all the talking. Either way, he planned to seriously consider life behind a desk as his next assignment. He thought about his brother, Zak, again and his job with The Organization. The name was pretty much all he knew, but he understood it was privately funded instead of government run. That alone was worth a looksee. Perhaps he'd consider applying there when he finished his career undercover with this lettered agency.

Then he went back to thinking about Jessica and where he'd take her the next time they went out. Dinner? Movies? Baseball game? All of the above? Or maybe she'd rather stay in and order takeout. That would be fine, too.

In his ear he heard Arthur's bodyguard call him up to the owner's office for a chat. He wanted to rebel and tell him to go fuck himself, but instead signaled he was on his way.

"I have a special assignment for you," Arthur said the moment Reece stepped into his lavish office.

"Okay. What's up?"

"I have a special guest coming in tomorrow night with several of his associates for a meeting with me. They'll be at the center court table. I'd like for you to be their personal security while they're inside the club."

"Sure. Who is it?"

Arthur narrowed his eyes. "Do you want their names?"

"Well, yes. How else will I know they've arrived so I can enter with them and keep guard while you all talk?"

His boss visibly relaxed. "Forgive me. This is a very important initial meeting for me and my new friend. Both sides want complete discretion, of course."

"Of course. I am the very definition of discretion." *As far as you know.* Although Reece thought it was stupid to expect any kind of *discretion* in a loud club when sitting center court. He did see an opportunity looming where Arthur would have to retrieve and enter new information regarding his new contact and the dealings. Perhaps Reece's work here was coming to a close.

Thirteen years ago—in his lucrative drug lord days—Arthur had always cleaned his own dirty money. Now he helped other criminals do it, for a hefty percentage. A multi-talented criminal with a huge hidden ledger with over a decade's worth of his best lawbreaking clients recorded. Somewhere. And the reason Reece was here.

"Honestly, you won't need his name," Arthur said. "He'll come with a very impressive entourage. You won't be able to miss them, trust me. This guest will be responsible for getting himself into the club under cover from the people waiting in line.

"Once he's inside, we'll use the curtains. In fact, I'd like their entire entrance to be hidden from the moment they come inside. From the vestibule, we'll have temporary drapery walls lining the ramp leading to their table."

Reece reflected quickly on whether this meeting would help him end this undercover gig, but said out loud, "I'll see to it personally. What time?" Reece made another mental list of all the hoops he'd have to jump through to make this circumspect meeting happen. He'd have to start setting things up tonight. It wasn't lost on him that Arthur hadn't given over the guest's name. And he wouldn't ask again.

"Late. Their arrival will be sometime after ten. They want the space until after closing."

"I can get it partially set up with the bulk of the heavy curtains tonight after we close."

Arthur nodded. "Good. Don't forget to run a bug sweep. Although with your girlfriend connected, maybe we're okay. As a matter of fact, why don't you ask her if anyone has shown any interest in watching this place recently?"

Reece faltered within. "Sure. I'll check it out. I'm

certain she would have said something if it were an issue."

He'd have to make contact and report this special meeting to his higher ups. They liked being apprised of any special guests Arthur brought in. This was additionally a significant boon because tomorrow night was the first time Reece would be the assigned security.

At long last he was being trusted. He knew it was because of his recent FBI connection to Jessica. He'd also have to tell Miles his suspicions regarding Elsa, Gordon, Neil and the freaked-out young blond guy who'd manhandled Neil inside the government car.

Reece had discussed it with Hector to get his read on that shady situation. He asked if Hector thought the FBI guy was trying to spy. The big bouncer had not hidden his laughter. "The dude had no chance to get inside this club *unless* he flashed his big federal badge. He just wanted in so he could scope out premium women. He would have had to hide that badge to get any further action, though." Hector laughed himself into a coughing fit.

If Hector was laughing Neil off, then he would also relay that sentiment to Arthur if asked. It helped that it wasn't the first time someone with a badge tried to get special entry privileges to impress others. The bouncer on duty notified everyone inside. In the case of Neil, he'd likely been after Jessica. Or Reece. Or both of them.

Later, Reece had further explained to Arthur that Neil's appearance was a personal matter regarding Jessica and not anything official. It had been an accurate gamble.

Once Reece got the center court set up for Arthur's new guests, he'd send a coded message through channels to give his chain of command a heads up regarding the coming private meeting. What they did with the information was above his pay grade. He'd be sent specific instructions through Miles.

He'd also inform them he'd stay close to Arthur after the meeting. His understanding was that whenever Arthur added a new client to his lists, he'd take a few days away from the club to enter them in his super-secret secure system. This was the very reason Reece had been planted inside this undercover gig for so long. The only person Arthur trusted completely was Dixon. Reece would have to watch him closely, too.

Dixon was an excellent protector and completely loyal to Arthur for reasons known only to the two of them. There was quiet speculation that Dixon might be Arthur's bastard. If that was true, Dixon took after his mother in looks.

Whatever their history, Dixon was rarely fooled. He was a good judge of character and was an additional layer of security Reece would have to get through or bypass. The latter was his better bet, as getting *through* Dixon to get to Arthur had never happened, to the best of his knowledge.

It wasn't a stretch to believe that Elsa and Gordon had planted bugs in the club. Perhaps even at the table he'd be guarding tomorrow night. He'd have to do a fake bug sweep and hope the muscle for the meeting didn't do their own check. They'd be stupid not to, but he'd seen it time and time again. Trust was often misplaced and humans were very fallible.

Reece wondered what might happen if he invited Jessica, Elsa and Gordon back to the club tomorrow night. The thought wouldn't leave his head until he'd texted her.

Want to watch me at work tomorrow night?
I can't talk, as I'm on guard duty at our table, but I can watch you *dance.*

Maybe Elsa can tear up the floor alongside you in the cheap seats.

Just a thought. Let me know. R

If she took him up on it, she'd either been lying about her love of club dancing or she and her two friends had been up to something else the other night. There might be other possibilities, but those were the two top contenders.

Reece vowed to do anything within his power to help her, drawing the line only at undermining or completely ruining his cover. If that happened, his career in or out of the field would no longer be his decision to make, if he kept his job at all.

Jessica floated to work the day after the operation in Reece's club. Elsa and Gordon had been gone from her apartment before she woke up, but Elsa had sent her a text assuring her the van's recording equipment had been turned off once they left the club. She hadn't heard them leave, and they hadn't come in by the time she arrived at work.

Pierce wanted her to attend an after-action meeting right before lunch to discuss the operation. She hoped to talk to Elsa before seeing Pierce to ensure no one else had been listening in on her fantasy date in the front seat of Reece's car. Just because it hadn't been recorded didn't mean her new boss hadn't heard them.

Neil hadn't been at his desk all morning. She was probably a terrible person for rejoicing in that little break from her nemesis, and she couldn't seem to wipe the smile from her face as she wrote up her report as to the previous night's op at the club. She didn't expect the little brown-noser would be gone for long, and she was right.

The good news was that right before Neil entered the floor, heading toward his nearby desk, Pierce had already parked himself in the extra chair by Jessica's desk. In his hand he held what looked like her report. Mostly he seemed to be there to deflect Neil. She was greatly appreciative.

When Neil saw them, a satisfied expression graced his smug face. One she had categorized quite a long time ago. It was the one where he was supremely arrogant after getting away with something yet again, thanks to his uncle's pull.

"You were right," Pierce said under his breath, staring Neil down from across the room. Clearly, he was unhappy about Neil's antics last night and equally unhappy to see him unscathed.

"I was?"

"Yes. Neil is proving more difficult to get off my team than I anticipated. I've been forced at gunpoint to allow him a second chance." Jessica didn't believe he was exaggerating about the gun to his head. That's likely what it took to get Pierce's compliance to allow Neil back on the taskforce.

"That's too bad," she said. "I was pulling for you to outrank his uncle. He'll always be a loose cannon we'll have to overcome in every situation where he's the least bit involved, in my opinion, anyway."

"That's my opinion, as well. Neil must have dirt on his uncle or else the man wouldn't be so forceful in his appeal to keep him not only employed, but on every high-profile case assigned within this building."

"So what have *you* been threatened with, at gunpoint?"

"Dire things I don't wish to repeat in the company of a lady, mostly because I'm the one who can't take hearing them out loud again."

She coughed to hide her laugh. "So his uncle didn't

buckle even after last night's near fiasco when Nimrod Neil showed up at the club?"

"Nope. And I explained *that* incident in great detail. He was unmoved. Said it was a mistake anyone could make. He also applauded Neil's proactive thinking for going there in the first place to help out his fellow agents, if you can even believe that load of bullshit." Pierce rolled his eyes and shook his head. "The two of them are useless and delusional, as far as I'm concerned."

Jessica nodded. "You're right. Neil must have a firsthand account of something juicy or a video. Movies can be very persuasive."

"That's the truth." He looked into her eyes with a sudden intensity she found difficult to look away from. In a low tone, Pierce said, "Here's another truth. I'll do my best to keep him away from actual teamwork, and not working with anyone else. If that fails, then I give you leave for whatever you need to do to defend yourself. I'll always back you up before, during or after any incident."

"Sir?"

"In other words, if that ass-kissing little prick gets out of line or touches you inappropriately, don't punch him in the throat. Kick him in the balls. It'll hurt more and dissuade him faster. Trust me. I'll take any heat for you."

She nodded again, stifling a laugh. "Thank you, sir. I'll keep that in mind."

Jessica had already planned to use Reece as a threat to keep Neil away from her, but having her boss back her up was huge.

For the next several days, however, Neil was on his best behavior. Even in the meetings with Pierce and the others, he didn't ogle her or make so much as a squeak to voice an opinion. Jessica was not fooled. It was only a matter of time before chaos reigned down around them.

She didn't expect he'd be able to keep this good boy

act up forever, and couldn't possibly depend on him turning over such a new leaf after only a single threat from Pierce.

The task force met daily to strategize and plan every possible tactic to catch their prey, with someone listening to the planted devices twenty-four-seven hoping to glean information. So far nothing of note had been heard.

Jessica got a surprising text from Reece late Friday night, inviting her to the club Saturday. Before responding, she called Elsa and read the text word for word over the phone.

"You must accept." Elsa's tone was excited.

Jessica balked. "Is it reasonable that you're still staying at my apartment?"

"Why not? I'm on a long spontaneous vacation. I notice he didn't invite Gordon again."

"Could be an oversight, or maybe it's because it's a Saturday night. If you aren't a girl, you aren't getting inside. Guys don't get in typically unless they plan to spend the vast amount of money needed to sit at a premium table, right?"

"True. Okay. We can still work with that. Any ideas about the VIP he's guarding in the premium space?"

"Nope, but I hope it's the guy Pierce is after."

"That seems almost too good to be true, you know?"

"I know. But if it's anyone doing anything they aren't supposed to be doing, we'd get a heads up either way, right?"

"Yes, right. One other thing, *chica*—you'll have to get out and dance with me. He's obviously expecting it."

Jessica's face went hot. "Is that necessary? Can't I just protect our purses and drinks while you get out there?"

"No. Trust me, two girls dancing together can get away with so much more than just one alone. We'll stay on the edge of the dance floor as close to the premium table your boyfriend's guarding as we can get. Text him back and accept his generous offer. Tell him I wouldn't let you say no. Meanwhile, I'll call Pierce and start strategizing. That will also mean we work all day tomorrow to get ready."

Jessica didn't have much enthusiasm when she said, "Awesome."

Elsa's trill of laughter came through the line, making her feel a little bit better. "I've got your back, *chica*. Not to worry. Tomorrow, I'll teach you some simple rocking hot dance moves that will turn heads, especially your guy's. See you in the morning."

Jessica quickly sent a text accepting Reece's invitation before she lost her nerve and had to explain her childish fears to her boss. It wasn't that she hated dancing, per se. She hated being the center of attention. She would loathe every moment of being on the dance floor. Then her memory of dancing with Reece filled her mind. He'd been perfect and kept her distracted while they moved around the crowded dance floor.

Thanks for the invitation.

Elsa is over the moon, of course, even though

Gordon left for home already. She says I have to dance with her.

She's promised to teach me something new.

I'll miss being attached to you while you lead.

But I'll enjoy it if you watch my new hot dance moves. J

When Reece confirmed, he said something about losing his job if he watched her too much, but that it would be worth it.

She had to calm her racing nerves over dancing alone with Elsa, hot new moves or not, *and* the idea of Reece watching her do it.

Chapter 12

Reece watched the dance floor without really seeing it. The meeting hadn't started, but he hadn't been allowed to guard inside the curtained area anyway. He also hadn't seen so much as the gender of the person who'd entered a few minutes ago. Arthur hadn't made an appearance, but that could be to allow his special guest to get settled in.

Earlier he'd stood at the entrance to the club, keeping a lookout for either Jessica or the person he was supposed to be escorting into the club for the *discreet* meeting center court no less. The word oxymoron circled his brain more than once. He'd stopped rolling his eyes, but decided they were utterly foolish. Guys like these yahoos tonight got high on their own power, and after escaping justice for too long, came to the erroneous conclusion they were untouchable.

He couldn't wait to prove them wrong.

The night was lively, meaning it was insane for a weekend. There were people lined up around the block to gain entrance. He'd reserved a table for Jessica and Elsa, but not in the premium section where he'd be. If she showed up after the special guests, Hector assured him they'd get inside without delay.

Reece didn't relish his role standing outside the curtains of the premium table. At least not yet, since Jessica wasn't here. Once she arrived, he'd have a great view of her table and the dance floor. He was anxious to see the hot new dance moves she'd learned. There was also a speaker nearby limiting his ability to listen in to any conversation in the curtained area to break his boredom. If he'd been invited to guard inside he might have been able to hear some of what they said, but would have missed watching Jessica dance.

He wished he didn't want to watch his girl more than he wanted to listen to these secret proceedings. For his part, he needed to stick with Arthur closely after the meeting. Something had been staged to help with that endeavor.

Reece knew the drill, even though this was technically his first time at VIP guard duty. Arthur would make an appearance, and Reece would have to pay attention to glean any information regarding the addition to his little black book of criminals or whatever was used. Even finding his method of recording his clients would be a boon. In addition to a lengthy life of crime in his younger days, and being a money launderer extraordinaire, Arthur did favors for people and fully expected favors in return. All contacts were supposedly entered into his super-secret system when he acquired a new special friend.

There had recently been an anonymous suggestion within his rank and file that perhaps Arthur was some sort of genius savant with the ability to remember infinite details of intricate deals forever without writing them down anywhere. And further, that the only recording system he used was his mega smart brain. In that case, Reece was screwed and so was the agency he worked for.

His mission was to find out what Arthur's system

was and do his best to thwart it permanently. The hardest part was waiting to be trusted while in the company of criminals and their various activities. Reece had never been so close to his goal. If Jessica's case helped him learn how the system worked, he'd be grateful and he'd ensure his higher ups knew it.

Tonight, he'd likely have to ditch her after making a big show of inviting her here. But the diversion he'd planned was to make Arthur feel threatened and then provide immediate protection, thereby staying at his side after this important meeting.

He hadn't given Jessica a specific time to arrive, and it was still possible she'd stand him up, but he didn't think so. Assuming Elsa and Gordon had planted bugs at the table as he suspected, Reece had pretended to do a bug sweep last night. He'd also commented to the security guy he'd enlisted to help him that it was a shame this premium table was going to be empty for the whole night until ten o'clock before the secret meeting Saturday night.

The guy had smiled and commented that at least Reece had a worthy girlfriend to bring in to enjoy it on occasion.

Later, Reece had done a real sweep and still found nothing. Maybe those listening to the bugs had clued into his hint and temporarily deactivated them to avoid detection. Or he was off his rocker and Elsa and Gordon were merely friends of Jessica's without ulterior motives. Either way, tonight should be interesting. He'd do well to focus on his own needs and not the fantasy of a conspiracy headed by his reluctant girlfriend.

Neither Jessica nor Elsa had arrived by the time two black vehicles rolled up to the entrance right before ten. The first was a huge SUV. Four large men stepped out the moment it stopped, as if they'd choreographed their exit in advance. Maybe they had.

They strode purposefully to the back of the second vehicle, forming a wide, two-man wall on either side, one of them opening the limo door. A figure emerged, opening a black umbrella as they disembarked. Two more alighted from the vehicle without any shelter. The four large men from the SUV walked alongside the person under the umbrella all the way to the front door. Hector had closed the rope, keeping those first in line back, standing in front of them as Reece opened the Lexicon's front door. He held it wide for the approaching group. One of the men from the SUV hurried two steps ahead to enter before the hidden figure.

Reece tried to get a glimpse of whoever had come out of the limo, without success. The umbrella shielded the person above his or her shoulders and the large men covered any further view. He didn't even see the person's legs. He waited until all seven had entered before walking in behind them to guide them to the center court table.

The figure beneath the umbrella remained hidden all the way. He saw two of the men take out bug detectors. Reece, directed to stand guard outside the curtains, hoped they weren't about to discover the place had been wired for sound.

No alarm was raised. The bugs must be turned off, if they were even there. Perhaps he was completely wrong about Jessica, Elsa and Gordon. But he didn't believe that.

The mystery guest had been inside for less than ten minutes when Reece saw Elsa just inside the main entrance. He searched behind her for Jessica, then realized she must have entered ahead of her friend. Remembering her first night here, Reece thought about the leather miniskirt and thigh boots that had intrigued him through the evening. Tonight, she looked so different he hadn't recognized her.

The visceral reaction to the dress she wore sent his pulse through the roof. A glance at a few of the males in the room told him both she and Elsa had been noticed. He couldn't leave his post, but had directed Sam to escort them to their reserved table near the floor by the stairs to where he stood guard. Reece did his best to keep his tongue from slipping between his lips to drool.

Elsa had a complicated hairdo with some sort of elaborate flower attached near her temple by some unknown magical means. She'd apparently done Jessica's hair as well, since she sported a similar hairclip, but without the big up do. Her dress was clingy enough to show off her amazing curves and made out of what *looked* like shimmering metal pebbles. It was short, like before, but instead of thigh boots, she wore sexy, black, fuck-me shoes with spike heels. To say she had stunning legs would be like saying the Mona Lisa was a nice painting, but it was the closest word he could think of to describe her.

Reece heard movement behind the curtain. He turned his focus from the dance floor as Sam led Elsa and Jessica to their table. If the meeting was already over, it was the shortest in the history of the club. He hadn't heard Arthur come in, although he could have entered from the opposite side, but he would have expected to see Dixon nearby at the least. With the curtains in place, he couldn't see the back hallway leading to the premium seating.

A glance back at Jessica's table. It was empty. He searched further. Sam was already on his way back to his perch by the front door. Reece's gaze shot to the dance floor and he saw her. She stared directly at him, arms in the air, her body undulating perfectly to the beat of the music.

He nodded to let her know he watched. She smiled seductively and kicked her sexy moves up a notch. The sway of her hips and lovely body hypnotized him for a moment. He cleared his throat a couple of times.

He heard more low voices from behind the curtain, only the murmuring was getting louder. The tone seemed cautionary at first and then more concerned. Shit. He hoped they hadn't discovered any listening devices. He turned from the dance floor and his sexy girlfriend to address what was going on at center court.

"No. Just stay here," said an over-loud, raspy voice. "I'll be fine. No one saw me come in. They won't know I was under the umbrella. I could be anyone. When Arthur gets his ass in gear and makes an appearance, tell him I'm on the dance floor with a hot bitch panting after me. And when I get lucky, he can wait until I've been satisfied."

The curtain closest to him parted suddenly, revealing an average-sized man with a wholly unconvincing and very cheesy comb-over. Reece wasn't an expert on the attractiveness of the male species, but he didn't think the guy had a snowball's chance in hell of getting any *bitch,* hot or not, to pant after him, let alone have sex with him. Although more often than not, money talked and everything else walked.

Mr. Comb-Over surveyed the dance floor as if he looked at a buffet, trying to figure out where to start first. "Fuckin' A. As promised, the women here are first-class and super sexy."

His eyes fell on Jessica and Elsa. "Look at those two hot bitches dancing together, will ya? Gives me a stiffy just watching them, you know what I mean?" He shot his bony elbow into Reece's arm twice, passing him by. "Hot damn, it's time to party."

The man clapped his hands, rubbing them together hard and fast, practically licking his lips as he descended a few steps and got closer to the dance floor. He called over one shoulder to his six-man detail, "Don't wait up for me. I'm headed into paradise. I'll be back when I get laid."

Reece looked on with horror as the VIP headed to exactly where *he* wanted to be. *So much for secrecy.* Four of Mr. Comb-Over's men followed, trying to surround him, which would look ridiculous in this venue, but the arrogant man waved them off. Jessica and Elsa were still dancing wildly. He shouldn't leave his post, but as the lead security person for the club, it was his duty to ensure idiots exactly like this bozo didn't harass the female guests.

"Sir," he called out loudly, speed-walking to the front of the pack to come alongside Mr. Comb-Over. "My boss will be out very soon to meet you. Perhaps you should go back to center court and wait for him. I'll have some appetizers sent up."

Reece half-blocked him from his intended targets, trying to herd him back behind the curtains, but the man was having nothing of it. He'd made up his mind to hunt for women.

"Out of my way." He pushed Reece's shoulder halfheartedly and put his lust-filled gaze back on Jessica and Elsa, moving toward them with his entourage following like faithful lapdogs looking for a treat.

Mr. Comb-Over suddenly started dancing, if one could call it that, jerking his hips from side to side erratically as he stumble-walked, snapping the fingers of each hand in the air to the beat of the music like some Greek Zorba, only with considerably less finesse.

"Hi there, beautiful girls," he said with a big goofy grin, swaying and slamming his hips completely out of rhythm to the music.

Reece watched helpless as the VIP moved closer and closer to Jessica and her friend. He scanned the room, looking for Arthur. He was the only one who could stop the madness of this particular freight train bearing down on them.

"What would you two girls say to joining me in my private booth?" He pointed over his shoulder to center court. "I have the best seats in this place."

Elsa narrowed her eyes, but didn't stop dancing. "That's very nice of you, but we'd like to keep dancing. Thanks anyway."

Reece relaxed, grateful that he wouldn't have to intervene. Elsa could probably hold her own with the likes of this ass.

Undeterred, Mr. Comb-Over then asked, "How about I make it worth your while? What would you and your friend say to a raunchy threesome with me upstairs? I promise that I'll pay you very well if I'm satisfied."

"Dude, I'm not a prostitute!"

Elsa had stopped dancing to shout over the din of the music. Jessica also dropped her arms to her sides. She'd gone motionless the moment the guy with the bad hair had propositioned them, wondering what would happen next. This was, after all, the man Pierce wanted. And he wanted him very badly. He'd mentioned in passing that he yearned for this man to hang, fry, get the needle, all of the above, or at the very least spend the rest of his life in prison, never again seeing a single ray of natural light.

When their target emerged from the curtained area, Elsa sucked in a surprised breath. She'd turned her body so that the micro camera mounted in her headband would face him. Jessica did the same. In her ear, Jessica heard Pierce say, "That's him. That's our guy. I wasn't sure about his voice, but I know that arrogant face. This is the guy we want. This is the guy we need to take down. Fuck me. I can't believe he's showing his face, the idiot, but it's good for us."

Reece followed the guy all the way to the dance

floor, seemingly trying to get him to go back to the curtained area. In the surveillance van before they'd even entered the club, they'd all watched the target arrive in the limo accompanied by very heavy security. They'd seen him make his way inside, hiding behind the umbrella and his men all the way. They'd heard every word he said before he left the safety and privacy of the premium center court seat. The bugs they'd used were state of the art, transmitting a different kind of signal than what most bug detectors used to find them.

Reece stepped between Elsa and the rude man. "Sir, please let me escort you back to your table."

He made a face at Reece, shoved him aside and suggested to the women, "What about a blow job? I won't pay you as much, but still, it would be worth your while." He grinned like he'd offered them riches far beyond what they could possibly imagine. Pierce wanted this guy to rot in prison. Having just met him, Jessica already wanted to kick him in the balls repeatedly.

Reece made a noise like an angry grunt. "If you say one more word to these women, I will escort you out to the curb," he said, inserting himself firmly between the three of them. "Besides, private entertainment has already been arranged for center court."

In her ear, Pierce said a few choice words about things he'd like to do to Cecil Bickley. Abruptly, he said, "Elsa, I want this guy, but do not go up there if sexual favors are expected. And if he tries anything, kick his ass."

Jessica was glad he felt that way. The only guy she'd be willing to have sex with looked like he was about to punch their target in the face and render him useless for their carefully laid plans.

Elsa leaned around Reece and said, "Listen up, dude. I am not having sex with you. Nor am I giving you a blow job. However, if you stop trying to buy sex and nicely invite me and my friend up to your premium space for a drink, we'll consider it."

"Sure. Okay," he said at the exact same time Reece said, "No! Absolutely not."

Reece glanced around the room as if searching for someone. Probably Arthur, Jessica surmised.

"Do not trust him," Reece said over his shoulder in Elsa's direction.

Elsa patted Reece on the shoulder. "I don't trust him. Guess you'll have to keep an eye on the both of us." She turned to Bickley. "This is my friend's guy. He's our bodyguard. He comes with us or we don't go."

Bickley gave Reece an annoyed onceover, then smiled. "Fine. He can come inside. What's one more muscle-bound guy taking up space?" He headed back to where he'd started, his four guards following his every step. Elsa and Jessica, Reece's guiding hand on her back, moved toward the stairs.

Before they climbed up, Reece whispered to Jessica, "I will not let him touch you. But be careful. Don't provoke him."

"I know you won't. I'll be careful. And trust me, I'd never provoke that ass."

One side of Reece's mouth lifted in amusement as they ascended the stairs to the premium table. Pierce remained quiet in her ear. The bugs Elsa and Gordon had planted were still working, but were turned off as she and Elsa entered center court through the curtain.

With all of them crowded into the curtained space, the area seemed small and confining. It was sheltered by gauzy draperies, looking somewhat like a sultan's tent only with popular music blasting through the filmy walls.

"What do you want to drink, honey?" Bickley asked Elsa. The leer was hard to miss, but at least he'd stopped propositioning them. Jessica didn't expect it would last.

"Champagne, of course," Elsa said with a sparkle in her tone. She sounded like a total party girl. Or at least what Jessica perceived as one. The day they'd met, Jessica got the impression Elsa was a very savvy, very competent agent. Apparently, she was also a superb actress when the need arose.

Bickley leaned in closer. "Geez, for champagne I should be getting my rocks off."

Elsa got up so fast she bumped the small table across the floor several inches. Jessica also stood, and swore she heard Reece growl. Or perhaps it was Pierce in her ear.

"Sit! Sit! Please, I was just kidding. You people are all so serious." Elsa inhaled deeply, put a stiff smile on her face as if she was *not* at all amused, and sat back down. Bickley whispered to one of his guards. Jessica heard him ask for the cheapest champagne available to be brought to the table. What a turd.

Their cheapskate host sat at one end of the horseshoe table. His entourage was lined up next to him like soldiers in formation. Elsa and Jessica were on the opposite side with Reece standing close enough she could feel his warmth against one shoulder.

"What's your name, honey?" Cecil put an elbow on the table, planted his chin on his palm and waited for her response.

"I'm Elsa." She nodded once at Jessica. "This is my friend, Jessica. What's your name?"

"Bickley. Cecil Bickley." He stated it like a British secret service agent with a license to kill. Jessica could practically hear Pierce roll his eyes from where she sat.

The waiter brought a bucket of ice with champagne already inside and three chilled flutes, and placed them next to Bickley. There was quite a production of getting the bottle popped opened, pouring bubbly, and passing the flutes around to Bickley, Elsa and Jessica.

"What shall we toast to?" Bickley asked with a big grin. Jessica was certain he was about to salute seeing their bare breasts tonight or something equally inappropriate. Elsa raised her glass first. "To new friends," she said, turning her gaze on Bickley as she added, "and second chances."

"Here, here," Jessica said quickly.

Bickley nodded and amazingly refrained from saying anything foolish. He lifted his glass and took a sip. The champagne tasted pretty good in her unschooled opinion. Perhaps even the cheapest champagne was good quality stuff in Arthur's favorite club.

Jessica glanced at Reece. His hands were clasped loosely in front of him, but his posture was rigid. No doubt he was ready for anything.

"What do you girls do when you aren't dancing in clubs?" Bickley asked.

"I'm on vacation, visiting my friend," Elsa said. "What do you do when you aren't asking women for sex every chance you get?"

Bickley's laugh sounded much like a donkey's bray. Jessica pressed her lips together and noticed Elsa's eyes widened appreciably at his amusement.

"I'm a businessman."

"Vague," Elsa said.

"Well, if I told you what I *really* did, I might get arrested." That *hee haw* sounded again and Jessica couldn't hide her smile. His laugh was so ridiculous.

Loud voices beyond the protected cocoon of the table stopped their conversation. Reece turned as Arthur and Dixon pushed past the curtains from a hidden opening on the opposite side of the dance floor.

"Arthur!" Bickley exclaimed. He stood to greet the Lexicon Club's owner, nearly knocking over the champagne bucket as he did so. One of his guards managed to keep the bucket from tipping over and spraying tiny ice cubes all over the floor. Arthur, Jessica saw, didn't look pleased.

"Sit down, Art. Let's talk some business. I'm long overdue for your particular services." That hee haw sound came again.

Arthur frowned. "Did you truly leave this protected space and go out onto the dance floor, Cecil?"

"What?" Was Bickley's constant state of confusion an act or was he truly clueless? Jessica would have guessed the latter, except that he'd managed to escape Pierce for quite a while.

Arthur pointed toward the club's wide dance floor beyond the curtains. "Did you go out on the club's floor and out of this space that you insisted had to be completely protected to safeguard your identity?" Arthur's gaze moved from Bickley to Elsa and Jessica. His eyes narrowed in recognition. His gaze shot to Reece before turning back to his perplexed guest.

Bickley puffed out his chest. "Well, I wanted some eye candy for my table." He gestured at Jessica and Elsa. "I couldn't buy any sex from them, but they agreed to have a drink." He shrugged like his bad behavior should be tolerated.

"I didn't go to great lengths to keep your identity hidden tonight so that you could promptly waltz out into the crowd to find women to decorate your table."

"We just want to drink champagne," Elsa said brightly, lifting her champagne flute. "You can have your meeting. We promise not to interrupt, don't we, Jess?" Jessica nodded.

Bickley put a hand on Arthur's shoulder. "Lighten up, Art. No one knows I'm here."

"Now they do."

He shrugged. "But nobody cares about me. I'm old news. You worry too much, Art."

"No. I worry exactly the right amount." He pointed to

Jessica. "She's an FBI agent. Did you know that?" Jessica felt the blood drain from her face.

Shit. Shit. Shit. How did Arthur know she was in the FBI?

Beside her Reece exhaled deeply as if shocked, and Jessica got her answer. A look at his face confirmed her suspicion.

Reece had given her up to his boss.

CHAPTER 13

"FBI? Really?" Bickley turned to Jessica as one of Reece's worst fears was realized. "No wonder she wouldn't blow me or take money for sex."

Reece could see it. Arthur was ready to kick Bickley to the curb for his incautious actions, at which point Reece's opportunity to discover how Arthur kept track of his contacts would evaporate like a drop of water in the Sahara.

Arthur paled in fury. "You are a jackass, Cecil. I will not do business with you." He turned away and Reece watched the best chance to cease this endlessly long undercover operation dissolve before his eyes.

"Wait!" Bickley grabbed Arthur's shoulder. "What are you doing? We can still do business. Why can't we?"

Reece abandoned Jessica's side, moving rapidly to step between the two men. He faced a suddenly fearful Bickley and said, "Hands off of my boss, Mr. Bickley."

The four men with Bickley swarmed around their boss, crowding Reece away from him. The table was knocked aside and the champagne bucket wobbled on its stand. Amazingly, the champagne flutes somehow stayed upright on the jostled table. It was a little comical to watch so many men trying to aggressively share the same small space and protect their clients.

Arthur raised his arms and shouted, "Stop! Everyone stop right now." Perhaps he foresaw an epic battle of the bodyguards and the bouncer that might ultimately level his favorite club.

Bickley shoved past the two guarding his front. "It's fine. Back off. Don't crowd us." He tried to catch Arthur's eye. "Art, please. We can make this work, can't we? I really need you to take care of my money for me."

"Not tonight. And stop talking about your money, for heaven's sake."

Bickley put his thumb and forefinger together, brushed his lips and did a juvenile locking gesture. "Name the night. I promise not to invite any women." Reece noticed Jessica and Elsa's subtle reactions to this change in plans. Bad news, obviously. Was someone listening in on their conversation? Undoubtedly. Or were they simply hoping to hear firsthand the gist of tonight's meeting? The other question that circled his brain was who the FBI was after, Cecil Bickley or Travis Arthur.

Reece has swept the whole area with his personal anti-bug instrument and found nothing in the way of surveillance. But the FBI could have turned it off until showtime. That would have been the best call. He'd personally invited the two women to the club, giving Jessica an opportunity to do exactly what she and Elsa had done—insert themselves into the private meeting. Well, they'd done it with Bickley's help. He'd also been invited, which hadn't hurt.

Given who Jessica worked for, it wouldn't be a stretch to believe they were both wired at this very moment. He hoped there were no further surveillance checks.

Arthur turned his attention to the two women, specifically, Jessica. "So tell me, is it safe to talk?"

Reece hadn't discussed with Jessica his undercover chain of command's plan regarding her being a dirty FBI agent on the take for Arthur's club. He looked over and tried to say sorry with his gaze, hoping she wasn't about to toss her champagne in his face.

Jessica didn't hesitate. She stared back into Arthur's eyes and said, "It is completely safe, so far as I can determine. I checked again before I came here tonight for any new operational chatter." She shook her head slightly. "There was nothing." She shrugged very convincingly, as if bored to even be asked about law enforcement involvement in the Lexicon Club. Reece was impressed.

Arthur visibly relaxed. "What about the guy who flashed his badge trying to get in here the other night? That was a bit troublesome."

Reece had already explained that to Arthur, but likely his hyper-suspicious boss was about to test their stories against each other. Fuck.

Jessica frowned. "Well, now. That's personal."

"What do you mean?"

She pushed out an exasperated sigh and rolled her eyes. "That agent *thought* he had a chance with me romantically. Trust me. He *never* did. He followed me here because he's jealous of Reece. He still believes he can win me over." She looked at Reece. "As if I'd give Reece up for anyone. The man is delusional. I am sorry if he caused any trouble for your club."

"No. Reece took care of it." Arthur clapped him on the shoulder twice. One big happy crime family once again.

Arthur turned to Bickley. "I still don't want to discuss business tonight, Cecil. Tonight was always going to be about getting to know each other and discover whether we could do business, not the actual meeting."

"Okay, so where can we meet? I got to tell you, Art, it needs to be soon. I've got a bunch of cash in desperate need of a shiny new home."

Arthur cleared his throat loudly. "Be that as it may, I will not discuss any business whatsoever tonight. We'll set another date in a few weeks—"

"A few weeks! Art, that's way too long," Bickley said. "I'm in dire straits here. I need your services sooner not later. You may not have been planning to do business, but I expected that we'd hammer out a deal tonight. I won't make it days, let alone weeks."

"Fine. Tomorrow night. We'll meet at a location that I determine later on. You'll get a text to your private number two hours before our meeting with an address. You may only bring three others with you. I'll do the same."

"Only three guards?"

Arthur shrugged. "You may bring guards, financial planners or hairdressers. I don't care. I'll be bringing my personal bodyguard and assistant, Dixon, and Reece and her." He pointed to Jessica. Reece blanched, but couldn't object.

Bickley seemed pleased. "Great. Guess we'll have some eye candy after all. That works for me. Wear another hot dress, will you, honey?"

"You want me there, Arthur?" Jessica laughed nervously. "Why?"

"Two reasons. First, I'll know the meeting won't be interrupted by any law enforcement assholes because if they *do* come in, I'll have to assume that you don't truly have *my* best interests at heart. Reece will promptly have to prove *his* loyalty by taking you out of the equation. Do you understand now?"

"That won't be necessary," Jessica said without a single glance in Reece's direction. "What's the second reason?"

155

He smiled unexpectedly with a surprising look of admiration. "I read about the robbery you foiled. You took down two rather nasty gunmen, shooting the gun out of one man's hand, as I understand it, and saved a hostage without killing anyone. I was impressed. I'd say you have exactly the skillset I require when going into a possibly dicey situation."

She lifted her glass of champagne. "Here's to kickass girls with guns, and also no law enforcement assholes showing up at your next meeting." She took a deep drink, closing her eyes for a few moments.

"Reece has been singing your praises, and he's a difficult man to impress. I'll have him contact you with the address. Or perhaps you two could come together."

She shrugged. "That's fine. I'll be ready." She took another deep sip from her glass. Did she feel like she'd just made a deal with the devil? That's certainly the way Reece felt.

Her eyes opened and her serious gaze found Reece. He felt unsettled. They were likely going to have an interesting discussion very soon. Her tight expression said she was unhappy. It wasn't a stretch to assume he might be persona non grata. At least he'd see her at the meeting tomorrow. Where he'd have to do his level best to protect her and ensure at the outset she wasn't wired for sound. He couldn't risk her getting caught with a wire.

Reece pushed out a breath, already hating the coming get-together. At the very least, he wished he could tell Jessica that he was an undercover DEA agent, knowing *that* would never be an option even after this was all over. He needed to carefully consider what he'd say to her. And more importantly, what he wouldn't.

Jessica discovered that not only did pure hell exist,

she currently lived there. As Arthur outlined his proposition for her to be present at the next clandestine meeting as his insider insurance policy, she had to pretend she'd been in on it the entire time. She'd managed to pull it off, so maybe she was a better actress than she thought.

In her ear, Pierce had been all over the place with his candid remarks. Ready to kill Bickley for his sexual overtures, and then elated they'd been invited to the hidden room without any sexual favors required, and then incensed when Arthur suggested Jessica would alert him to any possible operation in his club, cursing Reece and his assumptions.

He promptly calmed when Arthur invited Jessica to the very meeting Pierce wanted entre to for the sake of taking Cecil Bickley down. Pierce had told her to cooperate and pretend to be Arthur's inside *man*, as it were. Whatever it takes.

As Jessica made the final tribute with her champagne glass, she felt used by pretty much everyone. Pierce and the FBI as a start, but the more troubling source was Reece, who seemed to be making plans behind her back that she had to cover.

A horrible thought occurred to her. Perhaps he hadn't truly wanted her. Perhaps her connection to the FBI was the only reason he'd invited her back to his place for a second night and insisted he wanted to keep seeing her. Perhaps that was the reason he'd pushed so hard to stay with her because he could use her as a source for his boss and his illegal business.

He might not have instigated their first time together, but since he learned she was FBI, he'd worked very hard to keep her in his life. She had to close her eyes for a moment as shame and regret washed over her. Worst of all, she'd fallen for it hook, line and sinker.

If Reece had told Arthur she was keeping an eye out

to ensure the club wasn't under surveillance, then he was as guilty as his boss. She'd given him the benefit of the doubt up to now, but his duplicity hit her like a shovel to the jaw.

A glance at Elsa made her realize she needed to pay attention to her surroundings and lick her wounds later.

Arthur had been talking to Bickley, a conversation Jessica had missed entirely. He was already leaving through the curtained off area, his faithful assistant following behind him. Jessica hoped her wire transcript would be available to study later on. She hadn't heard any of the closing statements.

Elsa leaned in close. "Are you ready to leave, *chica*?"

"Yes. I'm past ready."

The two of them stood up.

"Where are you two going?" Bickley asked. "I got champagne and everything."

"Too much drama. We're going home," Elsa said.

Reece glared at him, then faced Jessica with an expectant look in his eyes. Was he sorry? Or was he only sorry she'd found out what he did? Maybe both.

Elsa stuck an arm through Jessica's and guided her out the way Arthur had exited.

Reece started to follow them, but Elsa glared at him. "We no longer need you for our bodyguard."

"Oh? Why is that?"

"We are leaving because it seems like you used my friend. Worse, you did it behind her back without so much as a whisper of warning. I know how I'd feel in the same situation."

His lips formed a grim line, but he didn't disagree or argue. "At least let me walk you out. Do you need a cab?"

"No. We don't need anything. Not from you."

In her ear, Pierce was cautioning Elsa not to play too hard to get. "We want him to chase after her."

"Jessica," Reece called out in a tone that sounded

hurt and bewildered, or perhaps it was simply filled with regret. "Please wait. Let me explain."

Pierce said, "Perfect. Let him explain."

They were on the ramp, still shielded from the rest of the club with translucent draperies.

Jessica gave Elsa a small smile and nodded for her to go on ahead. "I'll meet you inside by the front door in a minute."

Elsa gave Reece a convincing semblance of a wary glare, but moved away. Jessica faced him. "I don't remember having a discussion where I agreed to keep you and your boss apprised of any law enforcement sniffing around this club."

"I'm sorry, Jessica."

"Are you?"

"Yes." His gaze was filled with what seemed like genuine remorse, but she didn't trust it. Elsa was a great actress. Jessica thought she'd done pretty well herself, given that she'd been blindsided by Arthur's assumptions. Lying was easy, with the right motivation. That meant Reece could be just as talented at twisting the truth. "I didn't expect Arthur to say anything to you, especially not in front of others."

"And if he hadn't, I assume you would have continued to also not say anything, right?"

He looked up at the ceiling, shook his head and then gave her an intense stare. "The situation got out of hand. He asked me about you and I sort of—"

"You what? Told him who I was and then lied to him about what I'd do for you? You're lucky I covered for you tonight."

"I know."

"How did you ever think I'd do something like that? Because I won't warn him if there is ever any agency watching this place. I don't even have the clearance level for that sort of stuff." *Lie. Lie. Lie.*

His eyes narrowed briefly as if he knew she fibbed. "I was bragging about what you'd done in the café, saving your friend and your marksmanship, and that you were my new FBI girlfriend. Arthur was ready to make me break up with you, I had to say something. He decided it would be better if I could get you to spy for him. One thing led to another very quickly and—"

"And?"

"And he assumed too much. But by then I couldn't get out of it. I tucked it away and hoped he might forget."

"If he hadn't forgotten, were you prepared to ask me to help you defend this place from law enforcement sneaking in?"

One of his muscular shoulders lifted. "I was hoping it never came up again, to be honest."

"Naïve of you." She looked away from his earnest stare.

"Or frantic optimism."

She laughed, and heard the bitter note in the sound. "You don't seem like a man who ever gets frantic."

"I'm *agitated* about you coming to that meeting tomorrow night."

"Oh? Why is that? After all, I have the perfect skillset for your boss, since I'm a dirty agent on the take and all."

"I said I was sorry about that." His expression looked pained.

"I'm not ready to accept your apology yet."

Reece took a step closer. "But there is hope?" He gifted her with a very hot, sexy gaze, one that bored down to her bone marrow and melded with her DNA. They were close enough to kiss if either of them moved forward a couple of inches. Despite everything, she wanted to forgive him. He smelled so amazingly good.

"Please forgive me, Jessica," he whispered, his breath

caressing her lips. The loud beat of the club music pulsed inside her body.

In her ear, she heard Pierce say something to Seth. *Shit. Shit. Shit.* They were still listening in. She backed up a step, away from Reece's luscious scent and familiar warmth. He reached out, grabbing her arm. "Wait. Please."

Jessica saw the *frantic* in his eyes now. But was it because he was afraid of losing her or of losing his connection to the FBI? She wasn't prepared to deal with the answer.

"I need to go. Elsa is waiting for me."

"Please wait. I care very deeply about you, Jessica."

She whirled to go, then turned back and moved close. "Now see, I'm not certain I believe that at all. I'm troubled that after that very first night we spent together, perhaps I was merely a convenient way for you to get ahead at work and that's why you pursued me so very hard." Jessica was afraid to see the truth of her accusation in his eyes, so she didn't look for it. She marched toward the door, not expecting him to follow.

He practically body slammed her from behind, wrapping a strong arm round her waist, and pulling her against his chest. "That's not true and you know it," he said fiercely.

"Do I? Wrong. I'm fairly certain I never knew you at all." She tried to wrench herself from his firm grasp. "Let me go." He released her slowly. She still hadn't looked at him. He could be trying to trick her. He knew she was susceptible to his overwhelming masculine prowess.

She continued walking around the curve of the ramp with her gaze squarely focused on the front entryway. Elsa watched her descend. She and everyone else on the channel had heard the whole argument. She'd likely watched it as well. Awesome. Jessica Hayes, dirty FBI agent on the take, and complete naïve idiot in her love life to boot.

Hector smiled at Jessica as she walked by, making her pause for a moment for an additional lash to her self-esteem.

Absolutely everyone knew what a complete fool she'd been to ever think a man like Reece would not only be interested in her, but pursue her so doggedly. She remembered the level of her inexperience in matters of sexual satisfaction. *I'm the very definition of newbie sexual partner.*

If she'd had any occupation besides one that was law enforcement-related, Reece wouldn't have given her the time of day past that first night when he hadn't known anything about her.

She was a fool. Tears threatened to spill, but she refused to allow it. She sucked up her desolate feelings, shook her weepy attitude away, and headed for Elsa's car.

"I'm not certain what you're doing, Agent Hayes, but you'd better hope he doesn't break it off with you," Pierce said in her ear. "You *will* be at that meeting tomorrow. I don't care what you have to say or do to make it happen."

CHAPTER 14

Reece watched Jessica storm away with equally potent quantities of regret and relief. He didn't want her at that meeting. Cecil Bickley was unpredictable, roaming at will through the world with absolutely no impulse control. He couldn't be trusted.

Then again, watching Jessica walk away—after Arthur had opened his big mouth and outlined Reece's betrayal—was almost more than he could stomach. He wanted to chase after her, but heard a commotion behind him from the very source of his anger.

Bickley was on the prowl for more women. Reece figured the rest of tonight was about to be long and filled with more drama.

When the club finally closed its doors and he was headed to his car, he saw the late-night text from Jessica.

I know you're still working, but I wanted to say I'm sorry.

Maybe better than most folks, I understand having to do what is necessary for your boss, whether you like it or not.

I'll see you tomorrow night.

Text me the location and pick me up on the way. J

Reece was so grateful to be out of the doghouse, he forgot he didn't want her there. But her forgiveness was welcome. He'd simply have to remember that she was a trained agent with skills and then keep her safe regardless of what happened. He texted her back before heading home to his empty bed. He'd have to keep reminding himself that he didn't get to keep her after this assignment was over.

Reece tried to call Jessica around lunchtime the next day, getting only her voicemail at work and on her cell. He left a message, but she didn't call back. Instead, she sent a short text a few hours later mentioning a busy day. She made a point of saying she'd field his text whenever the meeting was about to go down and let him know whether to pick her up at the FBI office or her apartment.

Arthur had insisted on making the meeting late in the day, cutting into his shift at the club, but Reece wasn't upset about that. He was sort of hoping to be able to pick Jessica up at home and for his boss to choose a meeting place in town so they didn't spend the night driving.

Regrettably, nothing was going to go the way he wanted it to. Not tonight and likely not in the near future, either.

Arthur set up the meeting almost an hour's drive out of town. Jessica was still at work when he sent her the message, so he didn't even park, just texted her when he got close and slowed in front of the FBI building as she exited the front door.

When she got into his car, it was clear she was still upset. She didn't smile, kiss him, or even look at him. She fastened her seatbelt and looked straight ahead.

In a controlled tone, she said, "Let's go. You shouldn't linger here in front of FBI headquarters, it looks suspicious."

"I thought you'd forgiven me."

She glanced in his direction, but didn't actually look at him when she asked, "What makes you think I haven't?"

Reece pulled away from the curb, squealing his tires and making her hang on as he negotiated his way into traffic. "Well, let's see. You haven't looked at me, touched me, kissed me or smiled since getting in my car."

"I've only been in here for less than thirty seconds."

"I miss your smile." She purposefully didn't look at him. "And your kiss," he said under his breath, but loud enough for her to hear.

"Guess you'll also have to deal with regret." She pushed out a long sigh, kept her focus out the window, and added, "Let's just get this over with, okay?"

"We have a minimum forty-five-minute drive. It's a long time to spend in awkward silence."

Jessica shrugged. After a few minutes she said, "What is it you expect from me tonight? Or should I save that question for your boss?"

Reece tilted his head from one side to the other, stretching his tense neck muscles before answering. "The truth is I never wanted you at this meeting. If it were up to me—and it's not—I'd drop you off at your apartment. But since you're required to be there courtesy of Arthur, I expect he's going to want assurances that no one in any lettered agency is looking into his business. Can you provide an adequate answer for him?"

"Yes."

"Are you prepared to be very carefully checked for listening devices when we get there?"

She swung her head to stare at him for the first time since entering his car. "Of course." But her tone wasn't as confident.

"I'll try to be gentle, but I intend to be thorough," he

said with a grin, trying to loosen things up a bit. "I look forward to touching every inch of your body, searching for weapons or listening devices, even if your clothes are in place." He'd relish touching any part of her at any time. Arthur would insist on everyone being body checked completely anyway. He'd stop at a full strip search, but only barely.

Jessica didn't comment. She turned away to intently study the terrain outside in the fading sunlight as if there would be a pop quiz later.

"What is really up your ass? Why are you so mad at me?"

She shrugged, her gaze fixed out the window as if the scenery was a breathtaking spectacle. It wasn't. It was one broken-window-filled building after another on the edge of forlorn that should likely be torn down.

"Look, I need to know." *I want to know.*

Jessica's head whipped to the side and he got a glimpse of her profile. "You pursued me with only one thing on your mind and unfortunately it wasn't sex."

"That is not true! Wait. I didn't *only* want sex, but—"

She huffed. "I don't believe you."

Reece narrowed his gaze. "This seems like a trap where I can't possibly say the right thing, which is unfair." Did she think he was only after her because of Arthur? Would that generate so much anger? She acted like this was personal.

"Unfair? That's rich. I'm shocked you could get it up so many times for someone as inexperienced as I am in bed. You likely deserve a medal for successful and repeated performances. A big one. I can mention it to Arthur, if you'd like."

Reece had just merged onto the interstate, but slammed on his brakes and stopped the car at the side of the road on an iffy shoulder with his flashers going. Luckily, traffic wasn't heavy, but more than one car honked at him as they sped by their now stationary vehicle.

"Oh my good heavens! Do you have a death wish or something?" she asked, both hands clinging to the dashboard.

He snapped off his seatbelt and turned, almost climbing into her space. "Do you really believe that I'm faking my desire for you for the sake of my job when we're in bed together?"

Eyes wide, lips parted, she stared at him as if hoping the answer to that question was a resounding negative. "Perhaps the thought did cross my mind once or twice." She swallowed hard and appeared to be waiting, as if she needed to hear him tell her his innermost feelings. It wasn't something he was adept at, but the ludicrous idea that he wasn't attracted to her was...well, insane. He'd never once thought she was inadequate in bed. Why did she think such a thing?

His tone was a bit loud and aggressive, but he intended for her to hear him. "I believe I told you that I care deeply about you. I have felt this way since I changed your flat tire. Even so, I want to be with you. The truth is, I love you, Jessica. I can't even explain how much trouble even saying those words causes me on countless levels of my complicated and frustrating life, but it's the absolute truth.

"I never faked anything with you. Not once. Not ever. Nor will I. If you come away with anything else tonight, please be assured that you are it. The only one for me."

Finally out of steam, he twisted as he sat back down and put the car in gear. He reached for his seatbelt and watched the mirrors to assess traffic so he could re-enter the nearest lane. They were probably going to be late unless he sped there.

Her fingers landed on his arm. "Wait. I *am* sorry. I

mean it." When he looked at her, happiness and supreme relief filled her expression. "Turns out I'm more insecure than I thought about my general appeal and being a know-nothing virgin for our first time."

"You knew plenty," he whispered.

"Last night when Arthur called me out and assumed I was keeping the FBI at bay for him, I was caught off guard. I went straight to the idea that I'd obviously never be able to attract a man like you if you didn't want something else from me."

"A man like me? I'm nothing special." *I'm an undercover idiot who should never have admitted my true feelings out loud.*

"You are. Every woman in line to get inside your club is in love with you. I saw it when we entered together the other night. Every woman I've ever seen looks at you like you're their perfect fantasy man."

"That's not real. They only want something from me."

"Elsa said that, too. She tried to talk me out of my melancholy last night, but I was unconvinced. I was certain I was only a means to an end."

Never let her know you are undercover DEA. Especially never let her know that your higher ups wanted exactly that. Reece abandoned his seatbelt, put the car in park and faced her. "Are you convinced of how I feel for you, yet? Or do I need to prove it to you?"

Her brows narrowed. "How can you prove it?"

He grinned. "Come here and I'll show you. It's not like we haven't christened the front seat of my car before."

"We'll be late."

Reece laughed. "Oh, you think I care about that? You're so cute." He brushed his fingers along her cheek in a gentle caress. He wanted to grab her, pull her to his lap, and recreate the memory of their last sexual encounter, but settled down in favor of making up.

Jessica met him over the center console. Her mouth trembling, she kissed him like she was relieved. Reece took it as a good sign and kissed her back with as much passion as he could muster, which was a lot and might make them really late if he didn't release her and put the pedal to the metal for the rest of the trip. He didn't care if they were late. But he should.

As of earlier today, his DEA chain of command was ready to close up this undercover assignment. When he'd reported that he was close and explained all the details of tonight's meeting, they'd stepped things up in light of this new get-together with Bickley.

There was a team in place to take Arthur down tonight if he produced the means by which he collected his clients and their information. Bickley would also be swept up in the melee and turned over to the FBI.

Right before he picked Jessica up, Reece had learned that Cecil Bickley was a very high value target for the FBI. There was a unit gunning for him, but Reece didn't know who it was. Perhaps this was the special project Jessica had been working on. He wasn't sure. He kept the information on a back burner. No one save his handler, Miles, knew his role tonight.

Regardless of what Jessica said regarding the FBI following him—because they were—tonight would be a two-for-one special. There'd also be some interdepartmental collaboration if everything went the right way. It was the kind of cooperation that happened more often than the average civilian was aware.

She broke the kiss. "We can go back to your place tonight." *Maybe. If I don't wrap up this mission and leave. Or fuck it up with the same result.*

"What about Elsa?" he asked, retreating back to his own seat reluctantly.

She shrugged. "Maybe I don't care about hostess of the year anymore."

He nodded and secured his seatbelt. "Well, I'm probably supposed to go back to work after this, but since I'm not bucking for employee of the year either, I'm going to hold you to that afterhours party for two." *Unless everything changes tonight.*

He carefully pulled back into traffic, gunning his speed a little past the limit. He didn't want a ticket, but needed to make up a bit of time.

"How long do you think this will take?"

"No clue. It's my first time at this particular rodeo."

"Really?" She sounded surprised.

"I swear. Usually I'm just a security specialist, which means very good door opener, making it a completely glamourous job where women I don't care about fake their attraction to get inside faster."

Jessica turned partway in her seat to face him. She didn't speak for a long spell, as if trying to decide something.

Before he could decipher where her mind was at, Reece glanced in the rearview mirror and noticed a big, black SUV tailing him. If it was Elsa and Gordon or the FBI in general, that would be difficult to explain to Arthur, not to mention his chain of command. He should try to lose them, knowing his handler and on up wouldn't want the FBI's direct interference. It was likely foolish to believe the FBI *wasn't* in the middle of a plan to take Bickley down.

He sped up, using a few tactical moves to lose them. If Jessica had a tracker on her person, losing the SUV wouldn't matter. They'd follow. They'd better not interfere though. Both Bickley and Arthur had to reveal their criminal intent for this to be a success, not just one party. If the FBI jumped the gun to get Cecil before Arthur was proved complicit, the past year of Reece's life was wasted. Well, the part of the past year that didn't involve meeting Jessica.

Reece glanced at her. "Tell me the truth. Is the FBI following us?"

"What?" Jessica almost swallowed her tongue. "The FBI?" *Of course they are. How do you know?* "Of course not. Why would you ask?"

"I thought there was someone following us." He sounded matter of fact, but he couldn't know for sure, could he?

She turned to look out the back window, searching for the black SUV, but she didn't see it. "I don't see anyone."

"That's because I lost them."

Shit. Shit. Shit.

"Good for you." Acting like she was oblivious to anyone besides Reece was very hard work. And she'd already made a fool of herself because of rampant, crazy, girly insecurities that had no place in her frame of mind tonight.

Reece was a pawn in her mission to take down Cecil Bickley. That was the way she was supposed to look at him, but she found it nearly impossible. Once Pierce had learned for certain it was Bickley at the club, he'd been filled with something very near bloodlust. He wanted the man caught as soon as possible.

"At any fucking cost," he'd said repeatedly today.

In this case, the cost might be Reece. If Bickley produced dirty money for Arthur to clean, everyone in the room was going down. If they managed to get it on audio or, better yet, video, Pierce planned to storm in and take his long sought after target whether the business had been concluded or not. In fact, she wouldn't be surprised to see Pierce bust the door down, rip Bickley's still beating heart from his chest and take a bloody bite. He was downright scary where Bickley was concerned.

Perhaps her imagination was a bit fanciful, but Pierce had made his feelings crystal clear.

Failure was *not* an option tonight.

Reece placed her hand on his thigh, gripping her fingers as they drove to their destiny. It was possible Reece would become collateral damage. He might be arrested with Arthur, though Pierce didn't care about any of Arthur's offenses.

If Reece kept his cool and didn't make a big effort to protect or aid Arthur, she might be able to help him. She'd been surprised when Reece said he'd never before been a part of Arthur's illegal criminal activities or meetings with special guests looking for shiny new money. She planned to be a witness in his defense if he needed it.

He was a bouncer or rather a security specialist when he put on airs. He didn't know who his boss really was or what he did for a living, did he? Perhaps they could get Bickley without Arthur revealing his specific criminal activities. A pipe dream, certainly, but one she clung to.

Jessica had spent the day memorizing scenarios so that Pierce's greatest challenge could be addressed and his imminent arrest realized. Cecil Bickley had to go down tonight. Pierce had given her a very sophisticated ear bud. It wasn't as good of a transmitter over distance, so the FBI van had to stay close to be of any use as surveillance to record evidence of criminal activity. She also had some old-school technology in the heels of her stylish new government issue shoes.

Reece hadn't texted her the location, since he was picking her up, but Pierce had a contingency plan if the surveillance van lost her. He assured her he'd have more than one vehicle with an eye on her for this unusual field trip. A disguised Elsa and Gordon in a second vehicle were to stay ahead of Reece's car and lend backup assistance as needed and as they were able.

Pierce had been practically giddy with the idea that his dream of apprehending Cecil Bickley was about to materialize. If Bickley hadn't gotten off on a technicality during his last arrest and disappeared in the wind the moment he left the courthouse, Pierce wouldn't have been as dedicated.

Elsa told her Pierce had worked very hard to make a case the last time, but had been thwarted by a couple of foolish mistakes during a DUI arrest and sloppy processing by local authorities.

Jessica wanted the mission to be successful, and not just because Bickley was an ass.

Pierce, Seth and, if her bad luck held out, Neil, were in the SUV Reece had lost. Pierce hadn't wanted Neil in the same state during the takedown, but some sort of pressure was being applied. Apparently, Neil's uncle had made a firm request on his nephew's behalf to be at the conclusion of this particular mission so Neil could share in the glory of the arrest. Whatever.

Jessica figured Neil was due for a doozy of a mistake, likely of biblical proportions.

For Pierce's sake, she hoped Nimrod Neil held out until after the arrests before being his usual idiot self. Or perhaps Pierce had left him behind at FBI headquarters, bound, gagged and deposited in a broom closet as he'd threatened under his breath earlier. She'd love to see that.

The memory made her smile. Reece noticed and smiled back, giving her a look that said he loved her. Well, it was foolish, but she loved him too. It was especially foolish to recognize that at best, her bouncer boyfriend would have to get a new job tomorrow. At worst, he'd be in jail as an accessory to money laundering.

She shook off her fears and focused on all the many things Pierce had wanted her to remember for tonight's meeting.

"You know what I'm looking forward to?" Reece asked suddenly.

"What?"

"Make-up sex."

"Oh?"

"Last time we were together was pretty much the best sex I've ever had."

"Really?" She'd thought it was stupendous too, but convinced herself he was only faking his interest. There were still a few doubts circling her head, but she tried to banish them in the wake of his roadside confession of love. "Why do you think it was so great?"

He cleared his throat. "Because..."

Jessica thought every time with Reece had been amazing. Was it because she'd taken charge? Climbed on top of him in the front seat of his car? Done it in a public place?

"Because I've never had sex without a condom before." *Oh, yeah! How could I forget?*

"Oh, that?" She still had more than a week to discover if that spontaneous action would eventually result in that vision she'd had of her parents' front porch with her brothers lined up holding shotguns. No time to worry about it now. Time to focus on the task at hand.

"Yeah. That. Anything I need to be thinking about?"

"No. You don't have to worry about anything." *Not yet at least.*

"I see. Well. Good." He said the word "good" like he was disappointed. Did he want her to be pregnant? Surely not. But still, he loved her. Perhaps she wouldn't have to make that possible difficult trip to her parents' porch all alone.

Reece's phone, resting in one of the cup holders, started buzzing. He picked it up and glanced at the screen. "Interesting."

"What is it?"

He pushed out an annoyed sigh. "Another text from Arthur. He's changed the meeting place."

Jessica tried not to sound alarmed. "Why?"

Reece shook his head. "No telling. Maybe it makes him feel safer. Or perhaps he's a control freak who likes having others dance to his ever-changing tunes."

Shit. Shit. Shit. Jessica had lost track of Gordon and Elsa's vehicle when Reece pulled to the side of the road to profess his love.

If only Reece hadn't lost the follow on vehicle, too.

CHAPTER 15

Reece pretended it was no big deal to change the venue for the meeting, just a minor annoyance. But in fact, it was a huge fucking problem.

His team was in place. Resources had been expended. The higher ups in his chain of command would run their mouths about the cost overruns, as always. Then again, Arthur spent more than two decades as a drug kingpin in the Southwest before getting out of that business so he could go semi-legit as a club owner and part-time money launderer. There was a reason he'd been able to avoid prison all these years. He was a canny bastard.

Given what Bickley had intimated at the Lexicon Club about why they were meeting, Reece expected he was about to be added to Arthur's huge hidden criminal ledger. The one Reece was here to discover and obtain.

"Where are we going now?" Jessica asked. She was glancing out the back, perhaps looking for that tail he'd lost.

"Not sure." *I'm exactly sure.* "I need to call him and check something." *I need to call my team and warn them.*

He thumb dialed a number from memory. "Arthur?" he said into the phone, hoping she couldn't hear the person on the other end of the call. He was very glad he'd disabled the Bluetooth in this car to keep this conversation off the car speakers. "I'm unclear of exactly where this new meeting site is."

Miles answered with, "The location changed? Are you fucking kidding me? Where are you going now?"

"Well, after I take exit one fifty four off the highway, is it a left or right turn after that first stop sign that goes to the residence on Obsidian Lake?"

"You tell me. I know your FBI girlfriend is listening in," Miles said in an amused tone.

"Okay. Left and go a quarter mile to the blue house. Thanks."

"You got that right. Stay sharp. Once Bickley makes his pitch and Arthur records it—wherever he does— we're moving in. Also, we weren't able to contact the FBI and warn them off in time. They may show up, but they better not fuck us over. Just a heads up."

Great. More pressure.

"Got it. I should be there in less than twenty minutes. See you soon." Reece disconnected the call and slid the phone into his front shirt pocket, feeling like a big, fat liar. But he didn't want to take a chance on Jessica seeing the text from Arthur that had very explicitly detailed directions for the new meeting location.

"A house on the lake. Too bad it'll be dark soon. I'll bet the view is beautiful there."

Reece glanced at her. "Probably. But the view is definitely beautiful here."

She grinned. "Have you been to this lake meeting place before?"

"Nope. As I said, this is all new for me."

She put her hand on his thigh again. He covered it with his free hand. They didn't speak the rest of the way there. They just held hands. The drive was quicker than expected. He stopped at a gate with a keypad, retrieved his phone to punch in the six-digit number even though he'd memorized it. He did take the time to forward the message to Miles in case they couldn't otherwise get access to the lake house.

The gates slid open and he followed a paved road to the left and into the woods. Open fields of grass beyond the trees allowed quick glimpses of the lake as they drove the final way.

The sun dropped below the tree line and dusk settled over the wooded area as Reece pulled into the long driveway of the *only* house a quarter of a mile to the left after exiting.

The house was actually a faded blue, and looked in desperate need of some tender loving care. Or it had been made to look distressed like some high-end furniture he'd seen on television recently. People paid exorbitant sums for pieces that had been made to look like they'd gone through a war zone. To each his own.

Reece knew that Obsidian Lake only had a dozen or so houses spread out around its vast perimeter. Rich people lived here. Arthur knew lots of rich folks.

Since no one knew where Arthur lived, this was likely borrowed land from a friend or possibly another client, as was his typical policy during meetings of this nature. Or at least according to something Hector had said once in passing.

Reece opened his door at the same time Jessica opened hers. They walked silently to the front porch, climbed half a dozen steps, and he knocked on the rustic wooden frame.

"Reece," Dixon said in a flat tone the moment he opened the door.

"Dixon," Reece replied in kind.

Arthur's bodyguard gave a curt nod and stepped away from the door so they could enter.

"Right on time," he heard Arthur say from beyond

the hallway. "Join us, won't you? Your friends are already here."

Fuck. Who was already here? Bickley? He wasn't Reece's friend.

Dixon gestured for Reece and Jessica to precede him through the entryway on their left. Inside, the two-story log-lined room looked like an expensively faux rustic wood cabin, a far cry from the drab exterior.

Reece saw a stranger tied to a chair. Another man he didn't know was beside the first, also tied to a chair, but the second guy didn't look conscious. Was he even still alive?

The more pressing question, though, was who the men worked for. DEA or FBI?

Jessica followed Reece with Dixon at her back. Arthur had said their friends were already here, which she didn't understand because Bickley was not her friend.

She paused, but something hard and cold jabbed into her spine. She looked over her shoulder at Dixon's very sinister expression. He frowned and jabbed her once more with what felt like a big gun, nodding curtly in a silent order for her to keep moving. If it was a gun, a close-range shot would certainly put her in a world of hurt, assuming she survived it.

She moved forward another step and ran straight into Reece's unmoving back. Dixon nudged her again, harder. Her hands rose from her sides. She looked over her shoulder again. "Stop jamming that gun into my back. I can't go through him."

Reece tensed up against her when she said "gun." He also lifted his arms away from his sides, half into the air. What was going on? He moved a few steps further into the room and she followed, staying attached to Reece.

Jessica was halfway into the room before she saw the gagged men in the chairs. One struggled against his restraints, obviously panic-stricken. The other was unmoving.

Her arms came down. Tired of being poked in the spine, she leveled a dirty look at Dixon. Surprisingly, he backed off a little.

Arthur stood up across the room, and she saw he also held a gun. "That's far enough for now."

Reece asked, "What's going on here, Arthur?"

"That's the question I want to ask your girlfriend."

Her gaze locked for a moment with the struggling man's before she turned her gaze back to Arthur. Jessica hated this already, but pretended indifference. "I don't understand what's going on here either."

"Why were your friends here waiting at the first meeting site I set up? They were hiding out with scoped rifles, surveillance equipment and FBI badges."

She shook her head slowly, not feeling nearly as confident as she tried to appear. "I have no idea. I swear to you that I've never seen these men before. If they truly are FBI, I don't know them."

"Really? I'm not certain I believe you," Arthur said. He turned to Reece. "Unfortunately, your girlfriend seems to have a different definition of keeping us aware of anyone interested in my business."

"She told you she doesn't know who they are." Reece kept his gaze from her. She pressed even closer to his side.

"And yet two men with FBI credentials were waiting to spy on us."

Jessica saw Reece looked just as confused as she felt. "I did not betray you!" She took a step closer to Arthur. "Listen, I have never seen them before in my life. If they *are* FBI then they must be undercover and not on the books." She lifted her hands again in an exaggerated shrug. "I am not all-knowing and all-seeing where the FBI is concerned. No one is."

Arthur lifted his gun from where it had been resting at his side and placed it against the struggling man's forehead. "Then you don't care if I kill him." The other captive seemed to rouse, moaning and looking around as if only now realizing his predicament. His moans turned to shouts of protest beneath his gag.

Jessica shrugged. "Well, I'd rather wound and not kill people when firing my weapon, even though that's not typically protocol, but I don't believe I can stop you." She looked at both men struggling in earnest. They moaned loudly behind the gags, but any words they said were muffled. "Sorry, you two. I don't know how you got here. Wrong place, wrong time, I guess."

Arthur pushed the gun harder into the man's forehead, his gaze daring her to save them.

Jessica said the only thing she could think of. "Respectfully, sir, I question whether they are truly FBI agents at all, if you were able to apprehend them so easily. We are trained in counter surveillance. Maybe they aren't who you think they are. Either way, they are strangers to me. Do what you will."

Arthur lowered his brows and lowered the gun. "Interesting. All right. Maybe you didn't betray me. I'm sorry to have misjudged you, Jessica."

He turned to Reece. "What about you?" The gun came back up, this time against the second man's head. "What if I kill these two and dump them in the lake?"

Reece squinted at Arthur, unsure of the man's sanity. He'd never seen Arthur handle a gun before. "I'd rather not watch two murders, if it's all the same to you, but I also don't know these men. I can't honestly say that I care what you do with them."

He hoped these were not agents from his own chain of command. They'd been the only ones who had the information in advance. As far as he knew, the FBI didn't know where the meeting place was since he'd lost the black SUV that was tailing them.

Reece was also a little worried about the FBI credentials of the two men involved in this takedown if they could be picked up so easily. Jessica was right. Training in counter surveillance was a priority in their line of work.

Arthur pushed out a long sigh. "Why were they lurking around the initial meeting place? I only told a very few people about that location." Arthur started pacing. He suddenly turned and asked, "Do you think the club has been bugged?"

Reece shook his head. "No. I've swept that place top to bottom several times. If that's not enough, Bickley's men swept the center court last night before even sitting down."

They were interrupted by a loud knock at the front door. Arthur nodded to Dixon, who put his gun in the back waistband of his pants and went to answer the door.

Bickley and three of his bodyguards, strolled in. "Nice place you got here, Art. Bet it cost you a pretty penny," he said, looking around the large room.

When he registered the two men tied to the chairs, his attitude changed. "What the fuck, Arthur! What did you do to my guys?"

Arthur gestured with the gun in his hand. "These are *your* men?"

"Yeah. What's the deal?"

Arthur looked like he might blast Bickley in the head. "The deal is they have FBI badges, you moron."

Bickley laughed, the hideous sound reminiscent of a burro with laryngitis. "Those are fake creds, Art. I wanted to make sure no one bothered us, so I sent these two extra guys ahead to make sure the perimeter was secured. I guess it was."

Arthur pushed out a long sigh. He put his weapon in the drawer of a nearby desk and approached Bickley. "Plus, you could break my rules and bring more than three men."

"Well, I didn't think you'd ever know about these two extra guys, now did I?" He grinned like he'd gotten away with something and was extremely proud of it.

Arthur didn't smile, but he did look reassured. "Dixon. Untie these men and direct them outside. Rules are rules and Mr. Bickley is only allowed three. These two can lick their wounds away from our meeting. You're lucky I didn't kill them already."

"I appreciate your generosity, Art. I'm shocked they got caught. Maybe I'm paying them too much."

That hee-haw laugh was already getting on Reece's nerves. It was going to be a long night. Jessica's expression mimicked the way he was feeling—supremely relieved. At least they didn't have to watch anyone get murdered.

Arthur directed Reece to check Bickley's other men for weapons. They surrendered them and were added to Arthur's gun in the nearby drawer.

His boss sat on a small sofa in the center of the living room and directed Bickley to sit opposite of him on an identical sofa. In between the two sofas was a rectangular coffee table.

"Fetch us beverages, Dixon, if you please." Dixon left the room.

Arthur then motioned for Reece and Jessica to stand behind him. Reece couldn't believe the meeting was going to take place. He waited until Dixon came back with a rolling cart filled with coffee, tea, water, beer and wine. Once Arthur had a cup of coffee and Bickley had a beer, the meeting began.

Dixon sat in an overstuffed chair next to the sofa. Reece wondered if he was about to record the details, but he just sat quietly but intently studying the two men about to negotiate.

Arthur gestured to Bickley. "So, Cecil. What can I do for you?"

"I'd like for you to clean some money for me. I've been sitting on it for years. By rights, you'd think it should be laundered after all this time, but I don't want to take any chances."

"Where did the money come from?" Arthur asked and then sipped from his cup.

Bickley glanced at Jessica, took a swig from his beer bottle, and answered, "From the last job I did."

"Which was what? The method I use depends on where the money came from."

"Oh." Bickley seemed reluctant to say. "It was a job I pulled back in Chicago."

"A job? Explain."

"A scam. A fraud. Do you really need the details?"

"I'm afraid I do."

Bickley blew out a breath. "Basically I got authority over several large retirement funds and reinvested them in a private deal that should have paid off big. But unfortunately for the clients, the deal fell through with the exception of my salary and expenses, which had already been siphoned off."

"Are the funds in cash or some other form of asset?"

"Cash. All cash. And it turned out the Feds were onto me, but I didn't know it. They arrested me, but could never find the cash because I had such a good hiding place." He didn't elaborate. "The day it all came crashing down, I got off on a technicality for another minor offense, but the prosecution didn't have diddly. I would have gotten off anyway."

"And you believe the cash you have may be marked in some way?"

"It's possible. Unlikely, but I'm not completely sure. The FBI asshole after me back then was a very serious dude. I wouldn't put it past him to have found a way and copied the serial numbers on every bill."

"Do you have the cash with you?"

"Not all of it, but a portion is in the back of my SUV."

"What amount would you like to start with?"

"I have ten million with me." He talked about ten million dollars like he'd cleaned between the sofa cushions and found some spare change.

"When will you deliver the rest?"

"Tonight. I don't want to wait to bring it tomorrow."

"How much total?" Arthur asked.

"A hundred million, give or take."

Arthur took another sip of coffee. "My fee is forty percent."

"Forty percent?" Bickley let out a very long and loud whistle. "That's kinda steep, don't you think, Art?"

Arthur lifted one shoulder. "You are welcome to try someone else."

Bickley pushed out a long breath. "I have already. Seems forty percent is the going rate these days. Used to be more like twenty-five, back in the day."

"Inflation crosses all socio-economic boundaries."

"I'm desperate, so we've got a deal."

"All right. Dixon will show you where to unload the first batch."

"And then what?"

"Dixon will count it so we have an exact number and then he'll process it. While he works on what you have with you, you can fetch the rest of it." Arthur set his empty coffee cup on the table.

"No, I mean, when do I get my laundered money? What's left of it anyway." Reece thought Bickley seemed resigned to paying more than he wanted to, but would likely whine about it for the duration.

"I'll give you immediate access to six million tonight. Once the remainder has been counted and I have the exact balance, I'll provide you with instructions on how to access a special bank account with a balance in the amount of fifty-four million, give or take."

"How will you clean it?" Bickley promptly guzzled the rest of his beer and then belched.

Arthur's face shaped into a disapproving expression. Reece wasn't certain whether it was the ill-mannered belch or the questions regarding the laundered money. Maybe both.

After a long pause, he said, "That is not your concern, Cecil. Once I take possession of your cash and the exact amount has been verified, then I'll make the bulk of your exact share available in an off-shore bank account. Less my fee, of course."

"Of course."

"When can you fetch the rest of the cash?"

"Right now." He pointed a thumb over one shoulder. "I'll send my two extra beat-up guys to get it. We stowed it a couple of miles away with my sixth guy guarding it. It'll only take fifteen minutes or so for the retrieval."

"Excellent." Arthur turned to Dixon. "Do you have everything ready?"

When Dixon nodded, Arthur said, "Go ahead and get started on the first ten million. How long will it take to count and process?"

"Ninety minutes minimum. Perhaps as much as two hours with processing added in." Dixon left the room.

Reece waited for Arthur to pull out a ledger or make notes, but he only poured more coffee for himself.

Perhaps once all the money was collected, he'd whip out a flashdrive and a laptop to register Bickley as a brand new client. Bickley availed himself of the beverage cart, grabbing another beer, popping off the top and guzzling the first third of it like he was in a beer drinking contest.

Another thought occurred to Reece. Perhaps when Dixon *processed* the money, *that* was when the details were recorded. Arthur trusted Dixon like a son. He always had. Reece made a mental note to ensure Dixon was questioned thoroughly in that regard. Loyalty only went so far when one was facing prison time.

Bickley's men returned with a panel van filled with large, department store-sized shopping bags. Everyone exited the house and went into the first stall of the garage. The bags in the van were filled most of the way up with loads of banded money.

All of Cecil's crew started carrying oversized, white bags into the generous four-car garage. Reece was tasked with helping to transfer the money.

Full night had fallen, making Reece feel better about his team being hidden. They were close to the end. He could stop being undercover as soon as tonight, maybe.

The thought came with a sense of relief, along with a considerable amount of angst. Like he did every other minute or so since they'd arrived here, he glanced in Jessica's direction. She looked a little on edge. He'd noticed her surreptitiously watching him. He had no idea what was on her mind.

They had just finished filling a stall and a half with white bags. The back of the van was closed up and one of Bickley's men drove it away.

Dixon came back from wherever he'd been counting money and whispered something in Arthur's ear. Arthur nodded, his expression satisfied.

When the sound of several loud vehicles broke through the quiet darkness, his satisfaction turned to a frown. Twin shafts of light in the form of van headlights turned into the long driveway, followed by three other loud large vehicles.

The first van pulled into the driveway within sight of all the bags of money. The passenger door opened before the vehicle came to a complete stop and an FBI agent dressed in full tactical gear emerged and headed straight for Bickley. Another agent headed for Arthur.

Bickley's eyes widened to the size of saucers. He obviously recognized the man headed for him. "You!" he shouted and backed away.

"I'm Special Agent-in-Charge Pierce. Cecil Bickley, you're under arrest for so many crimes I'm not going to take time to list them all right now or we'd be here until dawn."

Arthur sent a scathing look at Jessica and Reece before saying, "I'm sorry—Agent Pierce, is it?—but this is private property. You have no jurisdiction here."

"I have a warrant in my pocket that says otherwise."

Arthur's face tightened. "Impossible."

"I assure you that it is very possible. This isn't *your* property, is it, sir?"

"No. A friend has allowed me the use of it. So unless you have a warrant for the property of the owner, Mr. Albert J. Jacobson, I'm afraid I'm going to have to ask you to leave."

"In fact, my warrant was issued with the cooperation of the actual owner, *Mrs.* Albert J. Jacobson, who was startled to learn her philandering husband had given you permission to use this place. Turns out it's her family home and has been for all of her life," Pierce said with a certain amount of satisfaction in his tone. Several of his agents had alighted from the numerous vehicles and stood behind him. Pierce said, "Arrest everyone, we'll sort it out at headquarters."

Reece stared at Pierce briefly and closed his eyes,

because he recognized him. He *was* an FBI agent. Unfortunately, he'd come onto this scene before Reece had a chance to figure out how Arthur recorded his numerous deals and clients. Not to mention that since he'd worked on a case with Pierce five years ago, the man knew exactly who Reece was, too.

As if he sensed Reece's silent cursing, Pierce looked at him and Jessica and started marching in their direction. It wasn't a leap for Reece to figure out the man must be her boss. Interesting.

Reece expected Pierce to arrest him personally. Instead, he stepped past Reece to go toe-to-toe with Jessica.

"I'll be arresting Agent Hayes myself. Turn around, Agent Hayes." He spun her, whipped out a pair of handcuffs and had them attached to her wrists before Reece could protest or offer any protection.

CHAPTER 16

"What?" Jessica had been so relieved the team had showed up she could hardly contain her jubilation or remember her part in the scenario Pierce had worked out. At least until he loomed over her with his imposing height, whipped her around, and snapped handcuffs on her wrists. That woke her up and made her pay attention.

Reece started to protest, but Pierce gave him a surly stare. "Don't even try it or I'll put you in cuffs, too." Pierce yanked on her arm. She stumbled alongside him toward Arthur.

Pierce stopped in front of the money launderer. "You thought we didn't know you were using her, but we did. Too bad for you." He motioned Gordon over to put the man in handcuffs.

She managed to give Arthur what she hoped was a convincing wide-eyed stare before she was led back to Reece, who looked angry enough to spit nails, but didn't interfere.

From an FBI van a few yards away, Jessica saw the side door slide open. Neil exited with Seth, the computer genius, hot on his heels. "Come back here, Agent Wiley. You're supposed to stay in the van," Seth said in an urgent tone.

Neil sidled up next to her, glanced down at her handcuffs and smirked. "You don't even know how many times I've pictured you this way, Miss Cherry." He made a kissy face near her cheek and grinned. When he turned, Reece was there. It was clear he'd heard what Neil said.

Reece took two steps right into the other man's personal space and towered over him. "Back away from her, Agent, or I'll bust your foul mouth wide open," he said in a low, dangerous tone.

Neil puffed up like a peacock. "You do that and I'll put you in handcuffs."

"You'll try to." Reece gave Neil a smirk that dared him to try it.

Arthur, Dixon and Bickley were handcuffed but hadn't yet been loaded into a van for transport back to FBI headquarters. Reece, surprisingly, wasn't handcuffed. Jessica had figured he'd be considered culpable for helping move the money into the garage. Perhaps Pierce was going to offer him a deal, since he knew they were dating.

Pierce noticed Neil standing in front of Reece. "What are you doing out of the surveillance van, Wiley?"

"I wanted to help you load the final prisoners. Especially her." He stared at Jessica like she was naked.

"Get back in the van. Now!" Pierce moved to stand in front of Jessica, with Reece blocking her from Neil's direct line of sight. She could make out his face in the narrow space between the larger men's shoulders.

Neil ignored the order and frowned at Reece. "I guess he's getting off scot-free because of his special connections."

Arthur stared at Reece, and his brows furrowed. Perhaps wondering why his bouncer wasn't also in cuffs.

"Shut the fuck up!" Pierce fairly shouted as Arthur asked, "What special connections?"

Neil sneered at Arthur, who was about to be led away by Gordon and Elsa, and said, "You're so stupid. He's been undercover in your club for a year. I know for a fact that he's with the DEA. You're totally screwed."

Jessica was possibly more stunned than Arthur. *Reece is DEA?*

The silence stretched until suddenly everyone was talking at once. Without warning, Reece punched Neil in the face, putting him flat on his back, decorating the ground.

Pierce grabbed Reece to keep him from dropping onto the prone Neil, who was screaming as blood ran down his chin, across his face and into the dirt.

"I agree," he told Reece. "You earned one shot, but I can't let you kill him even if he deserves it. And he does. Let me take care of it."

Sputtering and arguing over Reece's role in the op, Arthur, Dixon and Bickley were hustled to a waiting FBI van and driven away.

Reece turned to Jessica the instant Pierce released him. He opened his mouth and closed it without speaking.

"You're DEA?" she asked him.

Reece rubbed his forearm over his eyes once and then looked at her like he didn't want to say what came next. "No comment."

"That means yes, but you never once hinted that information to me."

He pushed out a long sigh. "Couldn't."

"Really?"

"Just like you couldn't share your secret operation with me, and I understood."

"You tattled to Arthur that I would help you."

"I said I was sorry about that. I swear to you no information that I gave him actually came from you."

Pierce, who'd remained silent for the duration of their conversation, chose that moment to intervene. "Turn around, Hayes. I only put the cuffs on you for Arthur's benefit. Now that Agent Wiley has fucked up Reece's cover, I guess I can let you go."

She turned on him. "You *knew* he was undercover?"

Pierce winked. "Well, I worked with him on a case five years ago. Things in his life could have dramatically changed, but I guessed he was undercover." To Reece he said, "I tried not to step on your case, by the way, idiot personnel notwithstanding." Neil, now sitting, held a hand to his bleeding nose and let loose a steady stream of bubbly-sounding curses. "Also, I know a couple of your brothers. Strong family resemblance there, you know? I would have figured it out, even if I hadn't worked with you before."

Jessica didn't know what to say about Reece, so asked, "Now what?"

Pierce rubbed his hands together, as if he couldn't wait to get started. "Once all of this evidence is collected, we'll prosecute some bad guys."

Reece grunted once. "*You* will. *I'm* screwed over. Somewhere nearby, my team is waiting for my signal."

Pierce cocked his head to one side. "What were you trying to find out?"

"We wanted Arthur's method of recording all of his clients and deals. This one deal won't give him the prison time he deserves."

The sound of another vehicle racing in their direction caught everyone's attention. Reece sighed. "I suspect that's someone from my chain of command about to unleash holy hell over this arrest tonight. The FBI was to be notified to back off."

Pierce crossed his arms, and said fiercely, "I wouldn't have backed off even if another gun had been to my head."

"Well, I've been undercover for a year at great expense for absolutely nothing."

"Maybe your chain of command will get rid of Neil for outing you," Jessica said. "That would be an accomplishment."

"Maybe. I'd like to watch at the very least. But not worth a year of my time."

A large black SUV turned into the drive, raced toward the house and slammed to a halt in front of them. Two men leapt out of the front seat.

"Who in the fucking hell outed my agent in front of the man we were trying to catch?"

Pierce, Jessica and Reece pointed at Neil.

"Hi Miles," Reece said.

Miles nodded once at Pierce and said, "We've met." The two shared a half smile before Miles marched over to Neil. "You're in a lot of trouble, Agent."

"Do you know who I am?" he asked, pompous despite the swollen nose dripping blood and mucus.

"Yeah, I do. You're about to be my bitch. Once I'm finished with you, I'll let the federal prison system have what's left of you."

"You're bluffing. My uncle—"

"Has already been arrested for allowing you to obtain inside information on my undercover agent," Miles finished for him. Neil blanched, his already pasty face going three shades lighter.

The man who'd accompanied Miles cuffed Neil and started reading him his rights. A struggling, protesting Neil was shoved into the SUV's backseat.

Miles turned to Reece. "By the look on your face right now, I'm assuming we didn't get what we needed."

"No. We did not."

"Not even a hint we can chase down or a thread we can unravel?" He glanced at his vehicle, where Neil was squirming in the backseat. "I'd take any crumb at this point."

Jessica said, "You wanted Arthur's criminal client list, is that right?"

Miles focused on her. "Yes. That and we needed his method of keeping track of his vast client network and all the dirty laundry he's done for them. We have no idea how he records it all or where those files are stored. Do you have thoughts on that, Agent Hayes?"

"What about Dixon? The more I think about it the more familiar he looks to me. Doesn't he seem familiar to anyone else?"

Miles shrugged. "Not to me. Where do you think you know him from? Does he have unlawful connections other than Travis Arthur, like a criminal place?"

"I don't know. However, I'm certain I've seen his face before. I just can't remember the context." Jessica stared at nothing, thinking furiously of where she might have seen Dixon before.

"If you think of something, I'd be grateful," Miles said. "I mean, he doesn't look familiar except that he's been Arthur's assistant forever. Who do you *think* he is?"

"I can't quite put my finger on it, but I know I've seen his face before somewhere." All three of them were staring at her with interest. "Some people can remember numbers, some people can remember names, but I can remember faces. I'll bet if you ran Dixon through facial recognition software, you'd find him in there as something besides a quiet assistant and bodyguard. Has anyone ever looked before?"

"Of course. He's been with Arthur for a couple decades. Whatever Arthur knows, I'm certain he does too, but he likely won't tell us a thing. He's too loyal. Do you think he has a criminal past? Something before Arthur? He must have been a kid. Maybe it's buried in juvenile records we can't see."

"I'm not sure. It's more of a feeling that he was

famous or something, but I can't remember. What can it hurt to check? A full scan can be done before he makes bail. If he's wanted somewhere else for a crime, maybe you can leverage him against Arthur."

"Good idea. We'll check into it." Miles looked at Pierce and smiled. "Some of your people are smart and helpful. Others are filled with self-important shit and need to be taken out like trash."

"Yes indeed. Feel free to keep Neil."

Miles laughed. "Trust me, I will. He revealed the identity of an undercover agent. He's going down. Unless his uncle sticks up for him."

"Thought you arrested him."

Miles lifted one shoulder. "I might have exaggerated that point. Although his uncle is in a big pot of hot water for confiding in Neil a private source. That's how dipshit knew about your identity," he told Reece. Miles looked at Jessica. "If you ever need a job, you come and find me."

"Not a chance," Pierce said. "Hayes stays with me."

Miles mouthed, "Call me," in Jessica's direction and laughed. He told Reece he'd see him at the debrief, climbed back in his SUV and drove Neil away, hopefully forever.

Jessica was suddenly very tired. "Do you need me to do anything?" she asked Pierce.

He allowed a smile to shape one side of his mouth. "No, not tonight. You're free to go. Reece, take her home."

She startled, unsure of her feelings for Reece at the moment. It wasn't a secret to anyone who knew her well that she didn't ever want to date anyone in law enforcement. The thought of how her brothers would go apeshit was enough for her to strike them off the list of potential boyfriends. More than that, she was well acquainted with how most guys in this line of work changed if their girlfriends were in the same life. They became overprotective. Jessica had enough of that already.

Reece as a hard-working bouncer was much more appealing than Reece as an undercover agent with the DEA. How could she focus on her career if his job would always take precedence over hers? And it would. She'd seen that happen, too. A lot.

Jessica allowed Reece to guide her to his car. She didn't say a word on the drive back to her apartment, and he didn't push it. He slowed his vehicle as they neared her building and she had her door open before it came to a stop.

"Wait," he said, grabbing her arm before she got too far. "Will you please talk to me?"

"I'm tired."

"Me, too. Let me come up. We can actually *sleep* together this time." His amused tone was comfortable and familiar and she loved him, but she didn't want another man dictating things in her life.

"I'd rather be alone."

"I see. Well, we still need to talk eventually."

"No. We don't. You were playing a part. It was a different part than I originally thought, but a part nonetheless."

"You're wrong."

"Am I?"

"Yes. If you want to be mad at me, fine, that's your right. But at least be mad at the fact I was likely going to disappear back into another undercover role after the arrests were made tonight and not because I was playing you. I wasn't."

"It's not that. It's just that I liked you better as a bouncer."

"Why?"

"I'm FBI. I'm career minded."

"Good. I'm all for your career in the FBI. But I will always worry about you."

She pushed out an irritated sigh. "Thanks, but I already have a father and four older brothers fighting for the lead in that overprotective position in my life. Barring the fact that I never wanted to date anyone in law enforcement, I don't need anyone else I have to fight so I can do my job."

"Maybe you don't, but too bad. I love you. I care about what happens to you. And it doesn't matter what either of us does for a living."

Her heart skipped when he said he loved her, but she forced herself not to give away her feelings. This was important. She had to be strong. "Oh? Why is that?"

"No matter what you did for a living, whether you were a kindergarten teacher or a bomb technician, I'd still worry about you."

"Because you don't trust that I can take care of myself."

"No. Not at all true. I've seen you in action—at the coffee shop, for example—so I know full well you can kick ass. But that doesn't preclude me from worrying. That's what love is to me. Deal with it."

His reference to the coffee shop brought clarity to something she'd wondered about. "You pushed me out of the path of that bullet."

"What?"

Jessica turned to face him. "You were the one who shoved me when that second gunman popped up like a bogeyman at a haunted house."

His hold on her arm loosened, but he didn't let go. "I did. Are you saying I should have let you take the bullet?"

"No. I'm grateful. I was out of my element that day, reacting as best as I could in the heat of the moment. You saved my life."

He shrugged. "I don't know about that. Maybe I only saved you from a graze to the arm. The crazy tweakhead firing at you didn't look like an expert shot to me."

Jessica closed the car door, cocooning them in his front seat again. "Okay. Say I love you, too. So what happens now?"

Though he smiled at the roundabout way she'd admitted she loved him, Reece drew his hand down his face. "I'm not even sure. My cover's been totally blown. There were so many witnesses, it's possible my covert career has come to an end. Maybe this time next month, I'll be behind a desk somewhere. Unless I find a new job."

"Does the thought of that upset you?"

He shrugged. "Surprisingly, only a little. Truth is, you already had me thinking about giving it all up."

"Really?"

He looked at her with an expression she recognized. A lusty half smile shaped his mouth. "Remember the last time we were parked in front of your apartment in the front seat of my car?"

Jessica felt her cheeks go hot. "Hard to forget something like that."

"That's the truth. Anyway, the idea of giving up my current career seemed inviting if I had something to give it up for. Too bad you aren't pregnant. It would be easier, knowing I had a kid on the way, to help make the decision."

Jessica sucked in a breath. "Who said I wasn't pregnant?"

"You did." His eyes widened. "I thought you said I didn't have to worry."

"Well. Not yet. It's too soon to know anything for certain."

His eyes narrowed. "So when you said I didn't have to worry, what did you mean?"

She answered his question with a question. "Are those regrets surfacing?"

"Maybe, but not about you being pregnant."

"Then what?"

He swallowed hard. "You mentioned having four older brothers, right? If you're carrying a kid and we aren't married, then I'm doomed."

She nodded, crossed her arms and smiled. "I'll protect you from them if it's needed."

"Good to know. One other thing you should probably be aware of."

"What's that?"

"My name is not really Mark Reece."

She let out a long-suffering sigh, but didn't mean it. "Bummer, since I already practiced writing Mrs. Jessica Reece in my diary a thousand times. What a waste of time." She rolled her eyes. "So what *is* your name?"

"Reece Langston."

She thought about it for a few seconds. "Okay. Mrs. Jessica Langston sounds pretty good."

"I think so, too."

She laughed. "Good. I want to make sure I get your name right when I tell my family about what you did to me. And, you know, for the birth certificate, should I need it."

His brows rose, but he didn't look unhappy. "Pregnant or not, I still want to marry you, Jessica."

"You do?"

"Yes. As soon as possible, if you're willing."

"I am willing. I do love you and since you aren't going to give me grief about my job I'd love to marry you."

He grinned. "Good. Elope or a wedding?"

"I'm the youngest of five and the only girl, as I may have mentioned. I'd probably get in more trouble for eloping than for having a child out of wedlock."

"I doubt that."

She bobbed her head in agreement. "Well, my mom might feel that way. Thinking about my brothers and also my dad's reaction makes me reconsider."

"You are making me nervous."

She laughed, delighted that he wasn't a criminal and that he loved her and wanted to marry her regardless of whether she carried his child or what job she had. In her mind, all the rest was just details. "I don't mean to make you uneasy."

"Yes, you do. And I get it. You want payback because I fibbed to you while I was undercover. I'm okay with it for a little while. Don't abuse it."

"Noted."

"So big wedding then?" he asked, looking more anxious than he had all evening.

"Let's elope."

He brightened like his life sentence had just been commuted. "Really? Are you sure?"

"I don't care about a big wedding. I care about you. Law enforcement or not, I just want you."

"Great. Tomorrow? Justice of the peace?"

"Perfect." Jessica had talked to her mother long ago, helping her brace for the fact she didn't want an elaborate wedding. Her parents had eloped too, for heaven's sake. Why did *she* have to have a big wedding?

"I love you, Jessica." He leaned forward and kissed her like he meant business.

"Are we recreating a memory here?"

"Not opposed to that, but I've never seen your bedroom. And I'd like to. Let's go upstairs."

"Okay. I guess." Jessica felt better about her future than she had in a long time. They walked hand in hand all the way to her apartment. As she opened her door, she added, "Before you come inside, I want you to know I'm also not housekeeper of the year."

After christening her bed with two rounds of incredible make-up sex the likes of which should probably be chronicled as the world's best sex ever, Jessica fell into a deep, yet slightly troubled sleep.

She wasn't concerned about Reece or their future, but she was disturbed that she couldn't remember why she knew Dixon's face. It ate at her, entering her dreams as a problem she needed to solve. Wasn't it her job to remember any and all faces? Hadn't she always felt like she was the best in her field? Hadn't she even won more than one award for this very skill?

A lightning bolt of previously elusive memory zapped her wide awake. She sat up in bed. Beside her, Reece stirred. "What's wrong? Bad dream?" He rubbed her back, soothing her for a moment until he seemed to fall back to sleep.

She got out of bed, opened her laptop and researched the memory she'd literally dreamed about. After only a few quick searches, she found what she was looking for and went to wake Reece.

"What's wrong? Another bad dream?"

"Get up. I need you to call your boss. I remembered."

"Remembered what?" He rubbed his eyes with the backs of his fists like a little kid.

"Call your boss. I have new information."

"You want me to call Miles?" he asked, but reached for his phone, cueing up his contact list and selecting one. He flattened back on the bed, looking like he was at least trying to be more alert.

Jessica heard Miles answer with a stern, "What the fuck do you want at this hour?"

"Jessica remembered something she wants to tell you. Be nice." He handed her the phone.

"Miles."

"Jessica. What's up?" he asked, sounding as sleepy as Reece looked.

"I remembered where I know Dixon from."

"That's tremendous. Good for you. Can I go back to sleep now?"

"He's got an exceptional memory."

"A what?"

"An exceptional memory. Like a savant with the ability to memorize complex things. He won the Exceptional Memory Championships a long time ago. That's where I know his face from. A kid from my hometown competed. He and his family got to fly to London, England and everything, but Dixon beat him that year. Only back then his name was Brian Bell."

There was a long silence on the line before Miles spoke again. "Okay. You have my attention. So you suspect that Arthur's method of keeping his vast files and contacts is his assistant Dixon and his exceptional memory."

"Yes."

"Thank you, Jessica. I've got to make a few late-night phone calls of my own now. Put Reece back on."

Jessica handed him the phone. "Yes. Yes, she is awesome. No, you can't, because I'm marrying her and taking some time off. What? Okay, then can I have the next two weeks off?" He nodded and winked at Jessica. "Excellent. Let us know what happens with Dixon and Arthur."

He hung up his phone and glanced at the clock. "Even in the wee hours of the night you are a hero. Now climb back in bed with me. You've earned the right to sleep in tomorrow."

Jessica snuggled up to Reece, grateful he loved her the way she wanted him to.

EPILOGUE

Two weeks later

Reece gripped Jessica's hand a little harder than usual, which earned him one raised eyebrow and half a smile. She winked at him. He loved this woman so much. They'd married in secret before discovering that she was in fact pregnant from that one time in the front seat of his car sans protection. A fact that they would neglect to share going forward.

Jessica wasn't convinced it was really happening, but he was. She'd done a drug store home test that was positive. She wanted to schedule an actual doctor's visit and then wait a minimum of three more months before telling anyone. That was fair, but it didn't change anything for him. He was so excited about the baby, he could hardly contain himself. Amazing to think how drastically his life had changed in such a short time. But he wouldn't trade any of it. He was lucky and he knew it. A fact he tried to keep in mind as they climbed the steps to her parents' home.

He was also lucky that his time undercover as a bouncer hadn't gone to waste since Dixon a.k.a. Brian

Bell had flipped on Travis Arthur in record time. Once they'd outed him as a member of the exceptional memory winner's club, courtesy of Jessica, he'd made a deal for a reduced sentence.

He'd never seen Miles so happy.

Reece hoped his luck wasn't about to end today. It was time to face the music, namely her four older brothers and her parents to tell them they'd gotten married. Next stop was Key West and the announcement to his family at the traditional biannual gathering. His mother would be ecstatic to have another daughter-in-law. His brother Zak had beat him down the aisle, but barely. Marriage seemed to agree with Zak and Reece had joined the happily married brother club.

"Are you ready?" Jessica squeezed his fingers.

"As ready as I'll ever be." He pulled her into his arms and kissed her like it might be the last embrace they ever shared.

"Relax. It'll be fine. Trust me. I won't let them hurt you. Besides, we aren't telling them about the baby yet, just that we got married. Okay?"

Reece shrugged. "Okay. Whatever you want."

She grinned. "I like when you say those three words best of all."

"Do you know what I like best of all?" He hooked an arm around her waist and kissed her mouth.

"Yes," she whispered, "but don't expect it to happen while we stay at my parents' house."

He pushed out a sigh. "I would never."

"So back to the baby. I don't want to tell them until after I see the doctor and know for absolute certainty that it's true."

He gave her a mock frown. "Oh, goodie, something else to look forward to."

"Regrets?"

"Nary a one."

"It's not too late to escape and go straight to Key West," she said, staring at her parents' front door.

"Yes it is." He lifted his hand to knock firmly on the door, but it opened wide before he touched it.

A man Reece recognized stood in the doorway. He gave Reece a hard look, squinting in recognition and then shifted his gaze to Jessica.

"Hi, kitten. Heard you were going to be here and didn't want to miss the chance to catch up. I'd first like to discuss a certain gun battle in a coffee shop a few weeks back."

"Do not start with me, Jackson."

"Is that any way to greet your favorite brother?"

Reece turned to Jessica. "FBI Assistant Director Jackson Hayes is your brother?"

"Didn't I mention that?"

"No. You did not."

Jessica put her hands on his chest and kissed his chin. "Would it have changed anything?"

Reece leaned in and kissed her forehead. "No. Not a single thing." He stared back at her brother and extended his hand. "Jackson. Good to see you again."

Jackson looked amused, but he shook hands and motioned them inside.

"What are you doing here anyway?" Jessica asked. "Or rather, who told you I'd be here? As if I didn't know already."

"I happened to call a friend and he mentioned that you'd been seeing someone. Also that you'd taken some vacation time after a big bust."

"Is this friend my boss, Martin perchance?"

Jackson shrugged. "No comment."

Jessica told Reece, "That means yes."

Reece grinned. "Do I get to call you 'kitten'?"

"No. You do not." Jessica scrunched her eyes in that adorable way she had. "Wait. How do you know Jackson?"

"We worked together several years ago." Reece had helped Jackson out, some would say he'd saved his ass, but he didn't expect it would translate into much goodwill when the other man found out he'd married his baby sister. Oh, and that he'd already gotten her pregnant.

He didn't have long to ponder that before a band of giants entered the room and swarmed Jessica. Reece was pushed aside like he was a ninety-pound weakling.

"Our little cat has come home," said one beefy brother, a sentiment two more echoed. After hugging each one of them, she said, "I'd like you to meet my new husband, Reece Langston."

Scary silence.

Three Hayes men sized him up like they were figuring the quickest way to tear him limb from limb for daring to invade sacred territory, namely, their only sister. Then Jackson slapped him on the back like they were old friends.

"Don't worry," he told his brothers. "I know Reece. We worked together once. Truth is, he saved my ass more than once. Since the four of us could never convince our little kitten to enter a convent, she's at least made a good choice in a husband."

With that endorsement, the three other brothers approached him with smiles and backslaps instead of trauma, hard feelings, and the removal of body parts. Reece gave Jackson a look of gratitude and considered any debt squared. A life for a life, as it were.

From across the room, a female voice said, "Jessica Rachelle Hayes! You got married without telling me?"

"Hi, Mom," Jessica said and rushed to be swept into the older woman's arms. The two of them hugged and started whispering, leaving Reece with all her brothers.

"Why do you call her kitten?"

Jackson smiled. "I was eight when she was born. The first day my folks brought her home to meet us, we all crowded around her bassinette. She took one look at the four of us and started crying, but she had this soft little cry. Sounded just like a meow. I told the boys our parents had brought home a kitten. The nickname stuck. She hates it. That means I enjoy using it all the more. Do you have any sisters?"

"Nope. Just a houseful of boys. I have four brothers, too."

"Well, good. Our little kitten will feel right at home there."

Reece relaxed, figuring he'd survived round one of meet the family—until her mother shrieked. "What? A baby, too?"

Jackson's hand clamped down on his shoulder and three more feral, shocked gazes rotated his way. "So. How long have you two been married again?" The feeling in his belly dipped. Jessica stared at him helplessly from across the room.

Reece grinned and winked. She smiled back.

It helped that *she* felt so protective of *him*.

Jessica ran across the room, leapt into his arms, wrapped her legs around him and said loudly, "I love him. I carry his child, and if you lay one single finger on him, I'll never speak to any of you ever again." She buried her face into his neck and kissed him like she might be pulled from him while the rest of them looked for a lynching rope.

"Relax, kitten. We've already established he's good people," Jackson said in a soothing tone. "No need to get all worked up in your condition."

Her head shot up. "Really? You aren't going to go native on him or anything?"

Jackson shook his head. "He really saved my ass, Jess. I owe him."

"Paid in full," Reece said quietly, hugging Jessica close.

When the Hayes patriarch joined them, it was obvious where the men in the family got their looks, though the burly tree trunk of a man quickly proved his daughter had his smile. He was clearly amused when he offered Reece, Jessica still wrapped around him, his hand. "If my daughter is happy then I'm happy." He turned stern. "Just keep her happy, right?"

"Right." What else could he say?

Her family was a lot like his—fiercely protective. That was the way it should be, in his opinion.

If this roller coaster ride was indicative of his and Jessica's coming life together, he couldn't wait.

Key West – a few days later

Reece pulled their two suitcases out of the taxi's trunk and rolled the luggage to the rear door along the brick sidewalk, checking over his shoulder several times to ensure Jessica was okay.

The weekend visit with her parents and brothers had been less traumatic than he'd expected. Having her eldest brother on his side from the get-go helped not only with the marriage announcement, but also with the unexpected baby news.

They hadn't killed him yet, so he counted their initial visit a success.

Jessica's numerous brothers reminded him of his own big family, making him all the more anxious to get to Key West for their biannual gathering.

He put in the security code and the lock released. He twisted the handle and opened the door. Turning to usher

her into the hallway beside the kitchen, he saw Jessica's worried expression.

"What's up?"

"This is a pretty nice place. Pricy, right?"

He shrugged. "I guess."

"Are you a secret billionaire?"

He laughed. "Sorry, no. I'm just a working guy. Problem?"

"No. Besides, you already married me and I don't remember a prenuptial agreement."

From inside, he heard his mother's voice call, "Reece? Is that you?"

"Hey, Mom! We'll be right in."

Jessica looked concerned again.

"We?" his mother said, arriving at the door as he propelled Jessica forward.

"Mom, this is Jessica. Jessica, this is my mom, Maura Langston."

"Pleased to meet you," Jessica said, sticking her hand out. Reece knew a hug from his mother was forthcoming.

"Great to meet you, too, Jessica. Reece has never brought a girl here before. What's your last name, honey?" his mother said, enfolding Jessica in her arms.

"Langston?" Jessica's voice trembled.

He watched his mother's eyes widen. "Reece? You got married? That's excellent!" Jessica's breath huffed out as his mother gave her another enthusiastic squeeze. "Now we have another girl in the family. Come on in. We were just about to sit down and eat. I hope you're hungry."

Reece grinned. His mother was happy to know they were married. She'd be over the moon when she found out about the baby.

"Who's here this time?" Reece asked.

"Full house. You go ahead and say hello to everyone, while I check on things in the kitchen."

Reece pulled Jessica into the dining room. Zak and his wife were the only ones in there. He heard the twins, Deke and Dalton, in the next room arguing with their eldest brother, Alex, about the best baseball team in the nation.

"Jessica, this is my only other married brother, Zak, and his wife, Kaitlin. This is my new wife Jessica. We eloped a little over two weeks ago."

Kaitlin cheered and jumped up to give Jessica a hug. "Yay! Another female in the Langston brood. And another elopement. Double, yay!" The two started chatting like they'd known each other since childhood.

"Congrats, bro," Zak said. "Think we're starting a fad with all the eloping?"

Reece shrugged. "Not sure. It worked well for us and it was better than a shotgun wedding." He winked at his brother.

Zak coughed. "Does that mean what I think it does?"

"If you think she's carrying my child, then yes."

Zak whistled. "Mom's going to flip. Wait to tell her when she doesn't have a dish of food in her hands or it'll go airborne."

"Noted." Reece punched his brother in the shoulder. "You don't have any announcements to make, do you? I don't want to step on your news."

"Not yet. And not for lack of effort."

Jessica and Kaitlin left to help Maura put food on the table. Minutes later they heard their mother unleash a single squeal of delight. Half a second after that, something crashed to the tile floor and that was followed by lots of laughing from the three women.

Reece entered the kitchen with Zak on his heels. A broken dish and lots of steamed broccoli covered the floor.

He looked into Jessica's amused eyes. "Can I just say that I love you even more, since I know exactly what you just told my mother and it's thanks to that I don't have to pretend to eat broccoli tonight?"

His mother grabbed him, kissed his cheek, hugged him, and kissed his cheek again. "I'm so excited about my first grandchild being on the way. You don't have to pretend to eat broccoli ever again."

Zak winked at his wife and said, "If I'd known that, Kaitlin and I might have been trying harder. Live and learn."

THE END

COMING SOON

BODYGUARD
BAD BOYS IN BIG TROUBLE 3

The baseball stadium is torture for Chloe Wakefield, from the noisy stands to the slimy man her colleague set her up with. Too bad she isn't with the sexy stud seated on her other side. He shares his popcorn. Shields her from the crowd. And, when the kiss cam swings their way, gives her a lip-lock that knocks her socks into the next county.

Goodbye, vile blind date. Hello, gorgeous stranger.

Staying under the radar is pretty much a job requisite for bodyguard Deke Langston, but he can't resist tasting Chloe's sweet lips. Nor her sexy invitation into her bed, where the sensuous little virgin proceeds to blow his mind.

But someone doesn't like how close they are getting. The thought that scares Deke the most is that another woman in his care might be hurt because of his past.

All of Deke's skills are put to the test as he and Chloe race to solve the puzzle of who is plotting against them.

Chloe's in danger, and Deke has never had a more precious body to guard.

BAD BOYS IN BIG TROUBLE

Nothing's sexier than a good man gone bad boy.

AVAILABLE NOW

Biker

Bouncer

ABOUT THE AUTHOR

Fiona Roarke lives a quiet life with the exception of the characters and stories roaming around in her head. She writes about sexy alpha heroes, using them to launch her series, *Bad Boys in Big Trouble*.

Find Fiona Online:

www.FionaRoarke.com

www.facebook.com/FionaRoarke